MAUREEN CHILD

CAPTURED BY THE BILLIONAIRE

Published by Silhouette Books
America's Publisher of Contemporary Romance

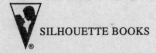

SILHOUETTE BOOKS

ISBN-13: 978-0-373-76826-4
ISBN-10:   0-373-76826-5

CAPTURED BY THE BILLIONAIRE

"I Own This Island And Everything On It," Gabe Said. "Including, At This Moment, You."

She stepped back and stared at him as though she'd never seen him before. Shaking her head, she whispered, "You can't be serious about keeping me locked up like this."

"Sounds like I'm serious to me."

She still looked damn good. He remembered the feel of her, the taste of her, and as something like hunger surged through him, Gabe had to admit that keeping her there had probably been a mistake.

She continued to stare at him, and Gabe almost felt a flicker of guilt. Almost. Then he remembered that one night ten years before, she'd walked away without a backward glance.

"I can do whatever I want to, Deb. This is my island. I make the rules."

Dear Reader,

Just imagine…the guy you broke up with ten years ago is suddenly back in your life. And not only is he as gorgeous as he ever was, now he's a billionaire! He owns the world's most fabulous resort—complete with his own island!

In *Captured by the Billionaire,* Debbie Harris and Gabriel Vaughn have a few things to work out. Like ten years' worth of anger and a whole lot of desire that's still simmering. So naturally, Gabe does the first thing he can think of to keep her on his island.

He has her arrested.

Not the fastest way to a woman's heart, but Gabe really had a mind of his own while I was writing this book. He even surprised me once or twice. Not an easy thing to do!

I do have to say, though, that during the writing of this trilogy, I absolutely loved the time I spent at Fantasies resort. It's everything a vacation should be. Romantic, opulent, seductive. Makes me want to pack a bag and head for the Caribbean myself.

I hope you enjoy your stay at Fantasies as much as I have!

Love,

Maureen

Recent books by Maureen Child

Silhouette Desire

*The Tempting of Mrs. Reilly #1652
*Whatever Reilly Wants #1658
*The Last Reilly Standing #1664
**Expecting Lonergan's Baby #1719
**Strictly Lonergan's Business #1724
**Satisfying Lonergan's Honor #1730
The Part-Time Wife #1755
Beyond the Boardroom #1765
Thirty Day Affair #1785
†Scorned by the Boss #1816
†Seduced by the Rich Man #1820
†Captured by the Billionaire #1826

Silhouette Nocturne

‡Eternally #4
‡Nevermore #10

*Three-Way Wager
**Summer of Secrets
‡The Guardians
†Reasons for Revenge

MAUREEN CHILD

is a California native who loves to travel. Every chance they get, she and her husband are taking off on another research trip. An author of more than sixty books, Maureen loves a happy ending and still swears that she has the best job in the world. She lives in Southern California with her husband, two children and a golden retriever with delusions of grandeur.

You can contact Maureen via her Web site www.maureenchild.com.

To Susan Mallery—
A great friend, a wonderful writer and a woman
who always knows just what to say. You're always there
when you're needed. Thanks for everything.

One

"Oh, God, I'm in *jail*." Debbie Harris curled both hands around the bars of her cage and gave them a frustrated shake. They clanked a little and the sound seemed to echo eerily around her. "I'm a *criminal*. I'll have a *record*."

Her forehead thunked against the bars and the fear at the base of her throat squeezed tight, nearly shutting off her air.

Okay, Deb, she told herself firmly, *get a grip. This is all a mistake. It'll be straightened out in no time. You're not in the Big House, for heaven's sake.*

In fact, the jail cell was more Mayberry than Oz. The whitewashed walls were clean and sparkling, and the cot was covered by a red-and-white quilt. There was a table and chair on one wall and a toilet and sink hidden behind a partition. The cell next to hers was empty and there was a closed door between her and the office where her jailer sat.

She scowled at the closed door because she couldn't do anything else. The man who'd locked her in here had been very polite but completely uninterested in listening to what she had to say. He'd simply closed the door to her cell and left her alone to wonder what in the hell had happened to land her here.

Outside the barred window, the tropical sky was a brilliant blue dotted with huge, fluffy white clouds, and the sun's rays fell in golden stripes across the red-concrete floor. She rested her forehead briefly against the cold bars and closed her eyes, remembering just how she'd ended up a prisoner.

After nearly four weeks on the private island, staying at the fabulous Fantasies resort, Debbie had packed her bags and headed for the tiny airstrip to go home. Back to her life in Long Beach, California. Where, it turns out, she should have *stayed*.

She'd filed through security along with everyone else leaving Fantasies that morning. The lines were long, even on this tiny island, as suitcases were checked while their owners moved through a metal detector.

Then she'd come to the Customs agent and everything had gone straight downhill. As he checked her passport, Debbie'd watched as his smiling brown eyes had gone flat and cold. He looked at her, checked her name again and frowned.

Interesting that despite knowing she hadn't done a

darn thing wrong, she'd instantly felt like a diamond smuggler or something. A wash of guilt and worry had smashed over her and when the agent motioned to a uniformed police officer to pull Debbie out of line, she'd felt the first jolt of real fear.

"What's going on?" She looked at the officer who had a firm grip on her elbow as he took her aside for questioning. "Is there a problem? Can you tell me what it is?"

He didn't speak until he got her away from the crowds. Now everyone thought she was a terrorist or something.

"You are Deborah Harris?" The officer's voice was quiet but no less demanding.

"Yes."

"American?"

"Yes." She avoided looking at anyone else, but she felt their stares on her. Lifting her chin, she squared her shoulders, looked directly at the man questioning her and tried to project an air of outraged dignity.

Not so easy to do when you were scared to death.

She wanted to shout, *I'm innocent,* but she had the distinct feeling no one would believe her anyway.

"There seems to be some difficulty with your passport," he was saying.

"What? A difficulty? What difficulty? It was fine when I got here."

"I can only say what I have been told by Customs."

"That's ridiculous." She tried to take it from him, but he whipped it back and out of her reach. Okay, this was fast moving from a little scary to downright terrifying. "Look, I don't know what's going on, but I've done nothing wrong and I've got a plane to catch."

"Not today unfortunately," he said with a shake of his head. "If you would please come with me…"

It wasn't an invitation.

It was an order.

Debbie seriously wished she had left Fantasies a week before, with her friends Janine and Caitlyn. If her best friends were with her, she wouldn't be worried. Janine would make some smart-ass remark and Caitlyn would be charming the Customs guy. Between the three of them, they would have had this all straightened out in a heartbeat.

But her friends were home, each of them no doubt all wrapped up in their wedding plans. God, it had seriously been a heck of a month. They'd come to Fantasies, the three of them together, to splurge on themselves.

Each of the three friends had been engaged and then dumped over the course of the previous year. So they'd decided together to take the money they had been saving for the weddings that hadn't happened and blow it on a treat for themselves. They'd had a wonderful time, until their threesome had slowly been splintered by the arrival of the loves of Janine's and Caitlyn's lives.

Caitlyn had ended up engaged to the very boss she'd come here to get away from and Janine…Debbie sighed wistfully. She'd talked to Janine only the day before and found out that her British lover had followed her home to Long Beach, California, just to propose. Now Janine was preparing to move to London, Caitlyn was planning the wedding her mother had always dreamed of and, apparently, Debbie was going to prison.

Sure. Her friends found love and she was getting a mug shot.

Life was fair.

"There's been a mistake," she said, digging in her heels when the officer, in his sparkling white uniform, tried to steer her through the terminal door. "If you'll just check again…"

"There is no mistake, Miss Harris." He was tall, with skin the color of smooth milk chocolate and brown eyes that looked at her as if she were an interesting bug. He was stronger than he looked, too. Her attempts at squirming out of his grasp failed miserably. "I am with the island security force. You must come with me."

"But my bags—" She flung a look over her shoulder at the bustling little airport.

"Will be retrieved from the plane, I assure you." His voice was musical, but there was no smile in his eyes. He kept walking, his grip on her elbow decidedly firm, just in case she should make a break for it.

"I'm an American citizen," she reminded him, and hoped that tidbit of information would do some good.

"Yes," he said as he tucked her into the passenger seat of a red-and-white Jeep. "I am aware."

While he walked around to the driver's side, she considered jumping out of the Jeep and making a run for it. But where would she go? Where *could* she go? They were on an island. The only way off was by boat or plane. She slumped in her seat and waited until he was sitting beside her to say, "What's going on? Can you at least tell me that?"

He shot her a sympathetic look, but shook his head. "I must report to my superiors. They will decide what to do."

"Who're *they?*"

He didn't answer her, just fired up the little car and steered it down the long road leading back to the village that spilled out at the foot of Fantasies. Wind in her face made her eyes water, but Debbie knew real tears weren't far off. Her stomach was churning, her palms were damp, and a tight knot of fear was lodged firmly in her throat.

She was on her own.

And she had had no idea what was going to happen next.

Sighing, Debbie came up out of the memories, looked around her and fought the fear still crouched inside. It had been two hours since the guard had locked her in this cell. She hadn't seen anyone. Hadn't been allowed to call anyone.

What were the laws on a privately owned island? Did she even *have* rights? No one was speaking to her. No one seemed to care that she'd been locked away. It was as if they'd turned the key and forgotten all about her.

"I could die right here," she muttered, looking now at the cozy little cell as if it were a dungeon with manacles hanging from its mold-covered damp walls. "Die and rot. No one would know. No one would wonder what happened to me and—"

She stopped abruptly and got a firm hard grip on her imagination. "For heaven's sake, Deb. Let's not get crazy here. Janine and Cait will miss you. You haven't dropped off the edge of the world. And you're not the Prisoner of Zenda or something. This is all a mistake. You'll be going home soon enough."

She sounded sure.

She only wished she were.

Voices drifted to her from the outer office. They were muttering, but at least she felt as if she wasn't alone on the face of the planet. "Hello? Hello?"

She grabbed her cell bars again and rattled them viciously. "Who's there? I need to make a phone call! I need to talk to *somebody*."

The outer door swung open slowly and Debbie took a deep breath. She was going to be firm. She would insist on speaking to the owner of the island. Demand that they straighten this mess out and let her go. No more feeling sorry for herself. From now on, she was going into battle mode. She'd been standing up for herself for years. And this was no time to quit.

She braced herself for whatever was coming. At least, she'd thought she was braced. But how could she ever have been prepared to see the man who walked through that door and looked at her through hard, green eyes.

He wore black slacks and a long-sleeved white shirt with the collar open at the neck. His long, sun-streaked brown hair hung loose, almost to his shoulders and when he smiled, Debbie felt a jolt of something hot and rich that she hadn't experienced in nearly ten years.

"Gabe?" she whispered, hardly able to believe her own eyes. "Gabriel Vaughn?"

"Hello, Debbie," he said, and his voice was as deep as she remembered it. "Long time."

She blinked at him and watched as he strolled casually across the jailhouse floor toward her cell. Despite her situation, emotions charged through her system, nearly battering her with memories and images of what she and Gabe had once shared. She couldn't help it. Just looking at his face was enough to wipe away the years between and remind her all too clearly of the last night she'd seen him.

The night he'd asked her to marry him.

The night she'd said no and walked away.

Now, his footsteps sounded loud against the concrete floor. When he came closer to her, the slanted bars of sunlight outlined him, keeping his face in shadow. "Looks like you've got some trouble, Deb."

"You could say that," she admitted, and when he didn't speak again, only stared at her, she kept talking, as though she couldn't stand the tense silence that stretched out between them. "It's all a mistake, obviously. I mean, I haven't done anything wrong…"

"Haven't you?"

"No." She didn't like the speculative tone of his voice, as if he were wondering just what kind of criminal she'd turned out to be. "It's some mix-up with my passport or something and they brought me here to talk to the owner of the island. But he hasn't come around and I've been here two hours already and—"

He braced one arm on the bars of her cage and looked down at her, with something like amusement flickering in his eyes.

"What're you doing here, Gabe?" she asked as a slow curl of suspicion unwound in the pit of her stomach.

"Here on the island? Or here in the jail?"

"Here," she said. "At the jail. Why're you here?"

"When there's a problem, I get called in to handle it," he said, lazily pushing away from the bars to wander back and forth in front of her cell again.

"Oh." Debbie's gaze followed him as he walked to the far end of the jail, then turned and strolled back again, like a man in absolutely no hurry at all. Of course, why would he be bothered? *He* wasn't the one in the jail cell. Impatience fluttered to life inside her. "So you're the police chief or something?"

One corner of his mouth quirked. "Or something," he allowed as he stopped directly opposite her and stared down into her eyes. "We don't really have a police force on the island. Just security. If we happen upon some real criminals, we hold them here until we can ferry them over to Bermuda. But the little stuff, we handle ourselves."

"And what am I?" she asked. "Small stuff or ferry-worthy?"

"Well, now, that's something we have to figure out, isn't it?"

"Gabe," she said quickly, "you know me. You know I'm not a criminal. Heck, I don't even *jaywalk.*"

His smile faded and he shook his head. "Ten years ago, I could have said I knew you. At least, I thought I did at the time…"

He let that statement hang there for a moment and Debbie knew he was remembering their last night together ten years ago. Just as she knew he wasn't smiling at the memory. She'd turned down his proposal, despite the fact that she'd loved him madly. She'd walked away from him when everything in her had yearned to be with him.

"Gabe," she said softly.

"But now," he quickly interrupted whatever she might have said, "who's to say? It's been a long time, Debbie. People change. Maybe you've become a master thief."

"I have not."

He shrugged. "Or a smuggler."

"*Gabe…*"

Fixing his gaze on hers, he said, "Look, bottom line, you're not going anywhere until the owner of the island says you are. He makes the rules here."

Debbie's hands tightened on the slick, cold metal bars. She wouldn't be getting any help from her long-ago lover. She could see in his eyes that he wasn't exactly thrilled to be seeing her again. So, fine. She'd handle this on her own. All she needed was five minutes with the mysterious island owner and she knew she could talk her way out of this mess. But it would help if Gabe would at least give her a little information on who she might be facing.

"So there's no police here. No courts. Just some rich guy who owns his own little universe?"

"Pretty much."

"So he's like a king?"

"He thinks so."

He gave her a quick grin and just for an instant her fear eased off. Gabe was a good guy. No matter how things had ended between them, she knew he'd never let her come to any real harm.

Of course, she *was* still in jail.

"Fabulous." Anxiety churned with anger and became a frothy, unsettling mix in the pit of her stomach. "Is he reasonable? Will he listen to me?"

"Probably depends on what you have to say."

"Damn it, Gabe, at least tell me what he's like. What I can expect."

A slow, lazy smile curved his mouth and his green eyes darkened until they were the color of shadow-filled forests. "I think you should expect to be staying at Fantasies for a while, Deb."

"What?" Her stomach dipped again and her mouth went dry as she watched his features tighten. "I can't stay. I have a life. A job. Responsibilities."

"All of which will just have to wait until you're allowed to leave."

Debbie snorted despite the trickle of fear dripping through her bloodstream. "Allowed to leave? What? You think the island's owner can somehow keep me here?"

Gabe lifted one shoulder in a shrug that said clearly

he didn't care one way or the other. "You're the one in the cell. What do you think?"

"He can't hold me in here forever," Debbie argued. "He can't just kidnap people and—"

"He didn't kidnap you," Gabe reminded her, "you came here on your own."

Her hands tightened on the bars. "And now I want to leave."

He grinned at her, but the shadows in his eyes remained dark, fathomless. "Hell, Deb, you're the one who taught me that you don't always get what you want."

Guilt pinged inside her despite her own precarious position. "Gabe, this isn't about us. But I can see that you're still angry about how we left things. And if you need to hear me say I'm sorry, then I am. Sorry, I mean. I wasn't trying to hurt you that night and—"

He laughed out loud, the sound rich and booming as it rattled through the tiny jail like a party with nowhere to go. Shaking his head, he said, "You're amazing, you know that? Deb, do you really think I've been pining away for you for the last ten years?"

Frowning and feeling just a little foolish, she said, "No, but—"

"I moved on a long time ago, babe." His gaze speared her. "Until you showed up here, I hadn't given you a thought in ten years."

Wow. That little dart hit home. Debbie didn't like knowing that he'd never thought back. Never remembered. But how could she expect differently? Just because she'd spent a lot of nights over the years, wondering if she'd made a huge mistake in leaving him…didn't mean he would have felt the same.

After all, it was *she* who'd ended everything between them. Why would he want to remember having his heart handed to him?

Gabe planted his feet wide apart, folded his arms across his chest and studied her for a long, thoughtful moment as his smile slowly faded. "You're right about one thing, though. This isn't about us."

Nodding, she told herself to let go of old times. To put the past where he had—behind them. All that mattered at the moment was the fact that she was in *jail*, for Pete's sake.

"Fine." Debbie let go of the cell bars, stuffed her hands into the back pockets of her jeans and rocked back on her heels. "Then why don't you tell me why the island's owner sent you here in his place? Why isn't he here himself if he's so interested in talking to me?"

"What makes you think he's not here?" Gabe's voice came low, a whisper of ice.

She looked past him, as if she could stare through the closed door to the outer office beyond. "He's out there? Then why…"

"Didn't say that."

Debbie's gaze shifted back to him and it felt as if there were a couple dozen lead balls rolling erratically around at the pit of her stomach. The truth slowly, inexorably, dawned on her and as it did, she noted that Gabe's green eyes went colder, darker, as silent seconds ticked past. "You mean—"

He stepped closer to the bars, looked her up and down, then his gaze locked with hers. "I *mean*," Gabe said, "I own this island and everything on it, babe. Including, at the moment, you."

Two

Her eyes went wide and horrified and Gabe wasn't ashamed to admit, at least to himself, that he was enjoying this. He could almost see her thoughts flashing through her mind as her features shifted from amazed to confused to fury all in the blink of an eye.

Of course, being Debbie Harris, it didn't take her long to erupt.

"Are you *nuts?*"

He laughed shortly. "Is that any way to talk to your jailer?"

She stepped back from the bars and stared at him as though she'd never seen him before. Shaking her head, she whispered, "You can't be serious about keeping me locked up like this."

But he was.

Gabe hadn't seen Debbie in ten years and he hadn't been lying when he'd told her he hadn't given her much thought in all that time. At least, he admitted, not until she and her girlfriends had shown up here on his island.

And from the moment he'd seen her, all he'd been able to think about was Deb. Irritating as hell, but there it was. He wasn't a man to be led around by his hormones and it was lowering to admit even to himself just how much he wanted her. After all, he had a life. A plan. And she had no part in any of it. And yet...

He let his gaze sweep over the bars of the cell before sliding back to her. "Looks like I'm serious to me."

She still looked damn good. The cute girl she'd been ten years ago had become a gorgeous woman. Her curves were lush, her long blond hair lay in soft waves down to the center of her back and her tanned skin was the color of warm honey.

He remembered the feel of her, the taste of her and as something like hunger surged through him, Gabe had to admit that keeping her here had probably been a mistake. Damn it, he could have been rid of her. She'd been at the airfield, leaving, walking out of his life again, yet when he'd been handed the opportunity—he'd had her stopped.

He still wasn't sure why, exactly.

"What kind of game are you playing?" Her voice was just a hiss of fury.

"No game," he said tightly. That much was true at least.

"Of course it's a game," Debbie countered. "Your

guy at the airport said there was a problem with my passport. We both know that's a lie."

"Not a lie. Usually, it's a ruse. Something the guards tell a suspect to keep them calm while they're being transported here."

"A *suspect?*" She shrieked that last word and then stopped, looked at him hard and said, "What do you mean *usually?*"

Gabe wandered the jail area, looking around as if inspecting the cells to make sure they were just as they should be. "It seems," he said quietly, idly, as if he couldn't be less interested himself, "there's a jewel thief working the resorts in this area."

"What does that have to do with me?"

He smiled and let his gaze slide up and down her body before spearing into hers again. "This particular thief is about five foot four, long blond hair, blue eyes…"

She swallowed hard, shook her head and said, "You can't possibly believe I'm a jewel thief."

No. He didn't. But when the notice from the British authorities had crossed his desk, he'd looked at it like a gift. Stupid. He couldn't afford to have her here. Especially now.

But he hadn't wanted her to leave, either.

One shoulder lifted in a lazy shrug. "You do fit the description."

"So do a lot of people."

"Yes," he said, smiling again. "But you're here. On the island. And we were asked to keep an eye out for a woman matching that description and detain her if necessary."

"Detain," she repeated, her voice sounding a little hollow. "Here? In jail?"

"If you're innocent," he started to say.

"If?"

"If you're innocent," he said again, "I'm sure this will be cleared up in a few days."

"Days?"

"Is there an echo in here?" he wondered out loud, hiding his amusement. "You'll stay as a guest of Fantasies until the authorities have been notified and proper steps are taken."

"What steps?"

He shrugged again and stared directly into her wide, scared eyes. "Fingerprinting, no doubt. You'll have to be investigated."

"You're kidding me. You don't seriously believe—" She moved up to the cell bars, grabbed hold of two of them and squeezed hard. "Gabe, you know I'm not a thief."

"No, I don't," he said reasonably, enjoying the heat of her temper. God, arguing with Deb had always been fun. "For all I know, you are this master thief the British authorities are looking for."

"British?"

He shrugged. "Apparently the thief ran through several estates in England before moving on to the island resort towns."

"I've never *been* to England," she argued.

Gabe smiled and turned to face her. "And I'm supposed to take your word for that?"

"Why wouldn't you?"

"I can't risk allowing a wanted criminal to escape the island."

"Oh, for—"

"So," Gabe said, walking toward her again with slow, measured steps, "until we get this straightened out, you'll be staying right here at Fantasies."

"You can't keep me here, Gabe." She stopped dead at the far end of the cell and glared at him.

"You're wrong about that."

She gaped at him and started pacing again.

He leaned one shoulder against the cold, steel bars and watched her as she stalked the confines of her cell. The heels of her sandals clicked frantically against the cement floor and the look she shot him should have fried him on the spot.

"I'm not guilty of anything and you can't hold me here against my will."

"I can do whatever I want to, Deb. This is my island. I make the rules."

"There are laws about kidnapping."

He chuckled. "Nobody kidnapped you."

She gritted her teeth, hissed in a breath and then spoke in a deliberately patient tone. "You can't just hold a person in jail because you feel like it."

He smiled, waved one hand to encompass the tidy jail cell and said, "Clearly, I can."

Sighing, she slid one hand through her hair, pushing it back from her face. "What's really going on here, Gabe? We both know I'm not this jewel thief, so why're you really doing this to me?"

There were too many reasons, he thought, and scowled as the humor he'd found in the situation moments ago drained away. He didn't owe her any more of an explanation than the one he'd given her. He had the right to hold her on the island until the authorities notified him otherwise. Still, if he kept her around for too long, things could get sticky.

He pushed away from the bars, stuffed his hands into the pockets of his slacks and said, "We can talk about this later."

"No, there is no later. I have a plane to catch."

"Actually, you don't," he said, watching her, "your plane's gone."

She just stared at him and Gabe almost felt a flicker of guilt. Almost. Then he remembered that one night ten years before, she'd walked away from him without a backward glance. And that memory was enough to steel him against the sheen of tears glittering in her eyes.

He only hoped it would be enough to help him hold out against the low, distinct throb of need pulsing inside him. "Look, as I see it, you have two choices," he said quietly. "You can spend your time on the island here, in this cell…"

She swung her gaze in a wide arc, taking in her surroundings in a heartbeat. He knew exactly what she was thinking. It didn't matter that the tiny jailhouse was a pleasant enough place. There were bars on the doors and windows and being locked away wasn't a good thing, no matter how nice the accommodation.

Which is how he *knew* she'd choose door number two when presented with it.

"Or," he said, meeting her gaze when she shifted it back to his, "you can come back to the hotel with me."

"With you."

"As the owner of the island, I can release you into my custody."

"Custody."

He grinned. "There really is an echo in here, isn't there?"

"Funny." Debbie watched him warily. "And if I'm in your custody, what exactly does that mean?"

"It means," he said, his voice low and dark, "you would be staying in my suite. Where I can keep an eye on you, until the matter is resolved."

"Why can't I have my old guest room back?"

Because he wanted her close, damn it.

"A wanted criminal?" he countered, lifting one dark blond eyebrow. "I don't think so."

"We both know I'm not guilty of anything."

"All I know is, you're in jail and I'm in charge," he said. "Up to you, Deb. Spend a few nights in a cell or come with me now."

She looked from him to the cot behind her and back again. She studied his face and said, "You're enjoying this, aren't you?"

"Shouldn't I be?" he countered, giving her a lazy smile that didn't even try to disguise his amusement.

Debbie stared at him for another long minute. She could hardly believe any of this was happening. Gabriel

Vaughn was the owner of Fantasies? The *owner* of his own, private island?

Ten years ago he'd had big plans and little else. Debbie had loved him madly back then, despite her own fears of a future that had looked shaky at best. Now, he was clearly more successful than even he had dreamed.

And she was literally at the mercy of a man who had every right to still be furious and bitter at the way she'd ended things between them.

This so didn't look good.

Her mind racing, Debbie tried to slow her thoughts down and slide them into some kind of order. By all rights, she should be on a plane home, having a tropical drink right now, served by a smiling flight attendant. Instead she was standing in a cell, facing down the man she'd once thought she would love forever.

But the truth was, she thought as she looked at him on the other side of the bars, she couldn't see anything of the Gabe she had known in the man watching her now. This man was cold. Even his smile was like ice.

She shivered, moved away from the cell door until the backs of her knees hit the quilt-covered cot behind her. Then she simply dropped to the narrow mattress and stared up at him. "I think I'll stay here," she said quietly.

Something in his green eyes flickered and she was pretty sure it was surprise. "You'd prefer a jail cell to the hotel?"

No, she thought wildly, somehow terrified of spending the night behind bars. "Yes."

"Fine," he said shortly, already turning for the door that led into the outer office. "If you change your mind, have one of the men call the resort."

"I won't change my mind, Gabe," she called as he opened the door and stepped through.

He stopped, turned his head to look at her and said thoughtfully, "You said that once before. A long time ago. But you changed your mind anyway. I think you will this time, too."

Then he left, closing the door behind him.

And Debbie was alone.

In the middle of the night, Debbie was wishing she were alone.

She sat up straight on her narrow cot and threw a furious look at the man in the adjoining cell to hers. The guards had brought him in an hour ago and he hadn't been quiet for a moment since.

"We will, we will, rock you!" The best that could be said about his singing voice was that it was loud. The worst was, he kept running through every eighties song his blurred mind could recall. And the words he didn't remember, he made up.

Debbie's head was pounding and her eyes felt gritty. She was so tired she could hardly think and knew she wasn't going to get any sleep at all. Not with the drunken lounge singer keeping her awake.

"Hey, honey," the man crooned suddenly as he leaned on the bars separating their cells. "Got any requests?"

"Yes," she snapped. "How about you shut up now?"

He grinned sloppily. "Don't know that one. How 'bout *'you're just too good to be true...'?*"

"Oh, God." Debbie cupped her hands over her face and sighed heavily while she was serenaded. She couldn't take this. Even facing down a cold-eyed Gabe would be better than being stuck in this cell with a drunk wannabe crooner.

Besides, there was no telling who the guards might bring in next. And with both cells occupied, the guards would start doubling up. Who knew who might be Debbie's roommate by morning?

Mind made up, she jumped off the cot, crossed to the cell door and shouted, "Guard! Guard!"

She'd never thought she'd be in this position. It was like she was living an old movie. All she needed was a tin cup to rattle across the bars. She was humiliated and scared and tired, and all she wanted to do was to go home. But since she couldn't at the moment, the hotel would be way preferable to life in a cage. Damn Gabe for being right.

When the security guard opened the door and looked in at her, she could have wept with gratitude. "Would you call Gabe for me? I mean, Mr. Vaughn?"

"What do you wish to tell him?" the man asked, pitching his voice to be heard over the strains of "Every Breath You Take," now being slaughtered by Debbie's cell mate.

She shot the drunk another furious glare, then turned back to the guard. "Tell him...tell him I changed my mind."

* * *

Debbie stepped into Gabe's suite at the hotel and could hardly notice any of the plush surroundings, since her gaze was locked on him. He wore nothing but a pair of black silk pajama bottoms that dipped low over his hips.

His broad, bare chest was tanned and sculpted as if out of bronze. His long, dark-blond hair hung loose and was tousled enough to tell her he'd gotten out of bed to answer her cry for help. The lights in the room were dim and the sheer drapes were pulled open, allowing the moon and starlight to drift inside on a wash of silver.

"Thanks for bringing her up, Emil," Gabe said, and shook the guard's hand before seeing him out and closing the door behind him.

Debbie stood in the middle of the living area and dared not take her eyes off of Gabe for an instant. When he met hers, she read annoyance and pleasure in those dark green depths and found herself shifting uncomfortably beneath his steady regard.

"Fine," she said on a sigh. "You were right. I changed my mind."

He leaned back against the door, folded his arms across his chest and crossed his feet at the ankle. Studying her for a long minute, he said, "I'm tired. It's been a long day. We'll talk about this in the morning."

"Okay, good," Debbie said, and finally took a moment to glance around her. "Just tell me where to sleep and I'll get out of your way."

"My room's through there," he said, pushing away

from the door and pointing to a door on the far side of the long room.

"Uh-huh. Where's mine?"

He smiled. "With me."

"Now wait a damn minute," Debbie said, shaking her head. "I didn't agree to—"

"Dial it down, Deb," he cut her off quickly. "Like I said, it's been a long day. I'm tired. I'm not arguing with you about this."

"Fine. I'll sleep on the couch."

"Don't have one." He started across the room, moonlight playing on his bare skin like a lover's touch.

"Don't have a—" She took a quick look. Chairs. Dozens of chairs sprinkled around the wide room, clustered in conversation groups, but no sofa. "What kind of a person doesn't have a sofa?"

"Me. Now come on."

"I'm not sharing your bed, Gabe."

"To *sleep,* Deb." He opened his bedroom door and scowled at her. "And you damn well are. I'm too tired to go chasing you across the island if you should try to escape."

"I'm not going to escape."

"Damn straight, you're not. Now come on."

Her insides squirmed uneasily. Sharing a bed with Gabe had not been a part of this deal. But she wasn't sure how to get out of it and, damn it, she was tired, too. After all, he hadn't been the one trying to sleep on a narrow, lumpy cot in a jail cell for the past several hours.

She started across the room, keeping her gaze fixed with his. "No false moves."

He choked out a short laugh. "Don't flatter yourself, babe. You're not that hot."

"Thanks very much."

"No more talking. Sleep now. Talk tomorrow."

"Fine."

She stepped into his bedroom and almost sighed. The room was huge, with an empty fireplace on one wall, a set of French doors leading to a wide stone terrace on another and floor-to-ceiling bookshelves on a third. An open doorway led to what must be the bathroom, and moonlight drifted in through the terrace doors, laying an invitation across a bed as big as a football field.

Every cell in Debbie's body groaned in anticipation. But as Gabe walked around the edge of the bed to the left side, she swallowed hard. He pushed those silk pajama bottoms down and off and stood there naked, watching her.

"Do you mind?" she said quickly, turning her gaze away, but not before her mouth went dry and her stomach did a quick spin and lurch. God, he was still gorgeous.

"You've seen me naked before."

"Yeah, but do you have to be naked *now?*"

He laughed, got into the bed and pulled the white duvet up over his hips. "Like I said, I'm tired. Now get into bed and go to sleep."

"I can't sleep with you naked."

"And I can't sleep with me in clothes. Guess who I'm more worried about."

"No guess required," she muttered, and walked around to the other side of the immense mattress. Stepping out of her sandals, Debbie thought seriously about sleeping in her clothes, but then decided that would be stupid. It wasn't as if Gabe was even interested in her. And if he did make a move, she could stop him.

Would stop him.

So keeping her eyes averted, she undid the button and zipper on her shorts and slipped out of them, letting them fall to the hardwood floor. Then she sat on the bed and swung her legs up.

"That's it?" he asked in a low-pitched grumble. "You're gonna sleep in your shirt and bra?"

"I'm very comfortable," she lied, laying her head down on a feather pillow that felt like heaven.

"Right. Whatever." He blew out a breath, rolled to one side and warned, "Don't try to leave the room, Deb. I'm a light sleeper."

"I remember," she said softly into the silvery darkness.

Whether he heard her or not, she couldn't be sure. And a moment or two later, she didn't care. She fell into sleep like a rock dropping into a well.

Three

Debbie sighed in her sleep, rolled onto her side and cuddled into the warm, hard body beside her. Her head nestled in the curve of a strong shoulder, she kept her eyes closed despite the wash of light she sensed beyond her eyelids.

Morning, and she wasn't ready to get up and go to work. Her mind drifted, focused and drifted again. She was just so comfortable she didn't want to think about moving just yet. She'd much rather—

"Comfy?"

She knew that voice.

Her eyes flew open even as she practically flew back and away from Gabe's warm, naked body. Amusement colored his features but something deeper flashed in his eyes. Hunger. She recognized it because it was sputtering into dancing flames inside her own body.

"What were you doing?" she demanded, shoving one hand through her hair while she scooted back to the edge of the mattress.

"Sleeping. What were *you* doing?" One corner of his mouth quirked into a half smile that tugged at Debbie's insides just as it once had.

God, ten years and he could still make her quiver with a look. What was it about him that she'd never found in anyone else? And how was she going to stay close to him without getting *close* to him?

What a mess.

"Nothing," she muttered thickly. "I wasn't doing anything I was just—nothing." She slipped out of bed, grabbed up the shorts she'd taken off the night before and tugged them up over her white lace panties. She didn't feel safe until she had those shorts zipped and buttoned.

For heaven's sake, she'd been practically laying on top of the man. All cuddled in like she belonged in his arms. He'd felt strong and warm and…safe. But hey, a person couldn't be held responsible for what they did in their sleep, could they?

He propped himself up on one elbow and the thick white duvet fell down his body to puddle just at his hips. Debbie closed her eyes tight and prayed he wouldn't move any more. She just wasn't up to another peek at a naked Gabe.

He grinned then, as if he knew just what she was thinking.

"If you're interested in a little morning wake-up, all you have to do is say so."

"I'm not interested, but thanks for the generous offer," she quipped, and hoped to heaven her voice didn't sound as shaky as it felt. "That—" she waved one hand at him "—didn't mean anything and you don't have to look so pleased with yourself." She swung her hair back from her face and tried to look a lot more self-controlled than she felt at the moment. "I was sleeping. Didn't realize that was you next to me and—"

"Ah." He interrupted her again and threw back the duvet in one easy motion.

Debbie swallowed hard, but refused to close her eyes. She wasn't going to let him know that his nudity bothered her.

Man, he looked really good.

"So what you're saying," he continued as he stood and stretched lazily, "is that in your sleep, you'll snuggle up to whatever warm body's available?"

"Yes." She frowned, distracted by the play of golden sunlight over his bronzed, rippled chest and abdomen and his hard and ready—*don't look.* "No. That's not what I—" She blew out a breath, forced herself to keep her gaze locked with his. "You're enjoying this, aren't you?"

"Is that wrong?" He grinned at her.

Debbie crossed her arms over her chest and tapped the toe of one foot against the gleaming hardwood floor. "Yes. *All* of this is wrong."

Staring at her, he reminded her, "You were the one cozying up to me, Deb. Wasn't the other way around."

"I'm not talking about that," she snapped, then sighed heavily. "Do you mind getting dressed?"

"Am I making you nervous?"

She smirked at him. Not for all the money in the world would she admit to him that he wasn't making her nervous at all—he was making her very…needy. "No. It's just not easy holding a conversation with a naked man."

One eyebrow lifted. "We don't have to have a conversation…"

"Oh, yes we do." Fine. If he wouldn't get dressed, she'd turn around. No point in making herself crazy by trying to avoid staring at all of that tanned, muscled skin. No tan lines, either. God. Did he sunbathe naked, too? Oo-oh. She closed her eyes and muffled a groan at the mental image rising up in her brain.

To cool herself off, to try to gather up the tattered threads of rational thought, she started talking again. "Last night, I agreed to come here because I didn't want to stay in the jail."

"So?"

"So…" Debbie stared at the painting on the pale blue wall opposite her. A beach scene at sunset, with deep, rich colors streaming across a canvas sky and drizzling onto ocean waves whipped by an unseen wind. "So how long do I have to stay here?"

She heard him moving around the room behind her and only hoped that getting dressed was part of his game plan.

"That depends."

"On?"

"On how long it takes for you to be cleared of suspicion."

"Oh, come on, Gabe."

When he didn't answer, she whirled around, saw that he'd pulled on those silky pajama bottoms, and blew out a grateful breath. Then she followed him as he walked out onto the tiled terrace off the bedroom.

The shining red tiles felt cold beneath her bare feet, but the sun was already climbing in a cloudless blue sky. In the distance, the ocean stretched out in front of the resort and flashes of colored sails on swift-moving boats caught her eye. Directly below them and to the left was a golf course, so deep and rich a green it almost hurt to look at it, and on the right, stone paths wound through carefully tended shrubs and flowers, leading to the pool area and the beach beyond.

"This place is amazing."

He swiveled his head to look at her. A brief smile curved his mouth then disappeared an instant later. "Thanks. I like it."

She smiled and shifted her gaze to the sweep of green where a couple of early golfers were steering a red-and-white cart down a path. "You used to talk about having a place like this. Remember?"

She flicked a glance at him in time to see his smile fade and a shutter drop over his eyes. "I remember. Look, Deb. I'm not interested in a forced march down memory lane, all right?"

"Yeah, sure." His instant withdrawal stung a little. But could she blame him?

He pushed off the railing, walked into his bedroom and threw words back over his shoulder like crumbs to a hungry pigeon. "I'll contact the authorities in Bermuda. See if they've got any more information on the jewel thief."

"Gabe, you know that's not me. Right?"

He stopped and glanced at her. "Doesn't matter what I know, Deb. All that matters is what you can prove."

"How'm I supposed to prove I'm innocent?"

Nodding, he acknowledged, "Good question. You should get to work on that right away."

"Aren't you going to help me?"

"I'm letting you stay with me."

She shot a look at the mile-wide bed and then looked at him again. "Yeah, about that. Is there a guest room—"

He laughed. "Why in the hell would I bother to have a guest room in my suite?" Shaking his head, he waved both arms and reminded her, "I live in a hotel, Deb. All the rooms here are guest rooms."

Good point. "Okay, let me have my old room then."

"No can do." He opened the top drawer of a sleek, polished dresser, pulled out a pair of black boxers, then slammed the drawer closed again. "As long as you're here, you're my responsibility. You stay where I can keep an eye on you or you go back to jail. You choose. Right now, I'm gonna grab a shower, then get to work."

She really hated this. Hated that she was caught up in something she couldn't control. Hated that she needed Gabe and *really* hated that he was so getting a charge out of giving her a hard time over it. And she hated knowing that she sort of felt *safe* with Gabe. She wasn't nearly as scared as she should be, because Gabe was right here, snarling at her. And looking way too sexy.

But she had no other choice. No way was she going back to jail. So she'd have to find a way to stay with Gabe without giving in to the feelings he could still inspire in her.

Sure.

No problem.

Oh, she was in serious trouble here.

"Fine," she said on a deep breath. "I'll stay."

"Glad that's settled. Call downstairs. They probably brought your bags from the airport last night."

"Okay, then what?"

He shrugged. "Take a shower. Get dressed."

"And then?"

"Hell if I know."

He turned to walk into the huge bathroom jutting off the master bedroom and stopped when she called, "But what am I supposed to *do* about all this?"

He sighed and said, "I'll make some calls later. See what I can find out."

"Thanks."

He didn't answer, just walked into the bathroom and closed the door behind him.

Alone again, Debbie looked around the empty room and wondered just how long she was going to be a prisoner in this palace.

* * *

"Jewel thief?" Janine's voice shrieked over the phone line and Debbie felt better just hearing her friend's fury. "Is he crazy? You're no thief."

Smiling, Debbie leaned back in her chair and took her first easy breath since being stopped at the airfield the day before. It was good to hear someone else's belief in her. "Thanks."

"Everybody knows you're too clumsy to be a jewel thief," Janine added. "You'd never make a living."

Debbie scowled at the phone in her hand and muttered, "Thanks again."

"Well, come on," Janine said on a laugh now, "you've gotta admit, jewel thieves have to be sneaky. You trip over your own feet."

"Okay," Debbie said, hoping to cut short Janine's amusement. "But let's pretend the authorities don't know that I'm a clod and figure out how I can prove to them that I'm not this thief they're looking for."

The restaurant by the beach was, as with most everything else at Fantasies, done in a red-and-white decor. White tables shone in the sunlight, red carnations sprouted from white vases in the center of every table. The servers wore Hawaiian-print shirts, also in red and white, and the crowd around Debbie was relaxed, celebratory.

As she had been only a few days ago.

That was, until she'd been arrested.

"Oh, God." Debbie stifled a groan.

"Right, right. But whatever happened to innocent until proven guilty?"

"Wish I knew."

Janine heaved a sigh that carried all the way from Long Beach to the beachside restaurant on Fantasies. "You say the owner of the resort is helping you?"

"That's what he says," Debbie told her, but privately she wondered. Gabe had no reason to be kind to her.

But she'd done what she'd believed she had to do to save both of them from more pain further down the road back then. Did she wish things could have been different? Of course. But that didn't change a damn thing, did it?

"You don't think he is?"

"I don't know." Debbie grabbed her glass of iced tea, took a long drink to ease the tightness in her throat and kept her gaze focused on the beach, so she didn't have to look at any of the other people seated in the restaurant. "I really don't."

She took a breath and blew it out in a rush. "Janine, it's Gabe."

A second passed, then…

"What? *Gabe?* You mean the owner? *Gabe?*"

"Yes, yes and yes."

"Oh, crap."

"Exactly." Debbie traced the tip of one finger through the water ring her iced tea had left on the glass tabletop.

"Is he still mad?" Janine asked.

"He says no."

"Well, of course he's gonna say he's not still angry. If he was still mad ten years later that makes him either a psycho or a big weenie."

While Janine ranted, Debbie's brain raced. Of course her girlfriends both knew about Gabe. They'd met him a few times back in the day, though she and Gabe had mostly preferred being alone back then. But her girlfriends had consoled her after the breakup and whenever she'd doubted the decision she'd made, they'd assured her she'd done the right thing.

"I can't believe Gabe owns Fantasies," Janine was saying. "And that we never saw him while we were there. Was he hiding? Is he hideously disfigured or something?"

"A million times no," Debbie said on a groan.

"Still hot, huh?"

"Oh, yeah."

"Well…" Janine's voice went thoughtful. "This puts a new spin on things, doesn't it?"

"Kind of, I guess. But the point is, I don't know what to do. Should I get a lawyer or something?"

"Beats me," Janine admitted, then offered, "I'll ask Max. Maybe he'll have some clue."

"Okay, good." That was something concrete. And hey, got them off the subject of Gabe and her own brief incarceration. "And speaking of Max, everything okay with you guys?"

"Only slightly wonderful," Janine said, and Debbie heard the near purr in her friend's voice. "He's helping me pack for the move to England—no, wait. Make that, he's paying people to help me pack."

"Works just as well."

"Yeah. He's really great, Deb. I mean, amazing and he's

gonna fly you and Cait to London for the wedding, which is turning into like a three-ring circus, by the way, because Max is this big deal in business over there and—"

"That's great, honey," Debbie cut her off without a qualm. After all, she was delighted her friend was so happy, but she had the little problem of oh, say, *prison* facing her at the moment. "But selfishly, back to me…"

"Right, right. Okay, I'll talk to Max. Then I'll call Cait. Maybe Lyon can do something, too."

Her other best friend, Caitlyn, was now engaged to her boss, Jefferson Lyon, who had plenty of connections in fairly high circles, so Debbie was prepared to take all the help she could get. Even if it was so damned embarrassing to have to ask for that help.

"Great. Fabulous. Now everyone will know I'm a felon." Debbie's chin hit her chest as visions of herself dressed in an old movie version of a black-and-white-striped prison uniform flashed through her mind. "I don't look good in horizontal stripes."

Janine laughed, clearly understanding exactly what her friend had been talking about. "Horizontal stripes are *nobody's* friend. Don't worry, Deb. We'll get this straightened out in no time. Until then, try to enjoy yourself. You're still at Fantasies. Make the most of it. And, hey, maybe you should make the most of being close to Gabe again."

Her body sizzled. Not a good sign. "That's so not gonna happen."

"Well, at least keep him *happy,* since he's the guy in charge of the jail key!"

"Right." She hung up, listened to the sigh of the waves rushing toward shore, the screech of the seabirds, and the conversations ebbing and flowing all around her. Enjoy herself. Sure.

No problem.

Gabe had plenty to keep him occupied. Even with a first-class manager and staff, there was work to be done. But doing that work while his brain kept circling around Debbie was no small task.

He knew damn well she wasn't a jewel thief. The only reason she was still on his island was that he wasn't finished with her. Yet. And if she thought she was trapped here, then so much the better.

Leaning back in his office chair, he swung around to look out the wide window behind him. His view of the golf course and the ocean beyond didn't soothe him as it usually did. Normally, he reveled in the knowledge that he'd made all of his crazy-ass dreams come true. He'd built an empire out of luck, talent and sheer grit, and he enjoyed the hell out of his life. It was everything he'd always planned for it to be.

But now, with Deb here on his island, he had the chance to settle a score that had niggled at the back of his mind for far too long. Ten years ago, she'd taken his heart and crushed it. Now, she was going to see just what kind of man she'd helped to create.

Ever since he'd seen her with her girlfriend down at the pool, he'd been thinking about her. Remembering things he hadn't allowed himself to recall in years. And if there was one thing he'd learned, it was that looking back served no purpose at all. The only thing that mattered was the present and the future you created for yourself.

Still…

There was a part of him that called for vengeance. Fate had handed him a golden opportunity and he hadn't become the success he had by ignoring quirks of fate. Besides, in that small, dark corner of his heart, he wanted to make Debbie sorry she'd ever walked away from him. And until he'd done that, he wouldn't let her go.

"Mr. Vaughn?"

His assistant's voice cut through his thoughts and Gabe turned to scowl at the woman standing in the open doorway. About fifty years old, she was tall, thin and so organized, she would have made a great general. She'd been with him for the last five years and probably knew even more about his businesses than he did. "What is it, Beverly?"

"There's a woman here to see you. A Debbie Harris?"

He smirked. Debbie never had been a patient woman. "Send her in."

Almost before the words were out of his mouth, Debbie was slipping past Beverly and striding into the office. "Thanks, Bev. That's all."

The woman sniffed in displeasure, but backed out and closed the door. When she was gone, Gabe fixed his gaze on Debbie and wished he didn't care about how good she looked. She was wearing a soft, blue sundress with thin straps over her tanned shoulders. The hem of the dress hit her midthigh and her heeled sandals gave her an extra inch or two of height. Her blond hair was pulled into a silver clip at the nape of her neck and hung in loose waves down to the center of her back.

And his only thought was, he'd like to bury his hands in that hair, pull her head to his and—maybe keeping her here hadn't been such a good idea after all.

"What is it, Deb?"

"Gabe, I need to know what you're doing about this." She moved around the office, trailing her fingers across glossy tables, stopping to peer at the jam-packed, rigidly aligned bookshelves and then moving eventually to the wall of windows behind him. She stared out at the opulent view and while she looked at the ocean, Gabe looked at her.

"I made a few calls," he lied smoothly. There was no one *to* call. The authorities weren't really interested in her. Her resemblance to the jewel thief supposedly running around the islands meant nothing to them. Gabe was the only thing keeping Debbie on this island. And she wasn't going anywhere until he was good and ready to see her leave.

"And?" she asked.

"And…nothing so far." He saw the helplessness glint in her eyes as he added, "The authorities are looking into the situation."

She shook her head slowly, sadly. "I can't believe this is happening."

A quick twist of something that might have been

guilt shot through him as fast as a lightning flash. He ignored it. "Don't worry."

"Easy for you to say."

Easier than she knew.

She chewed at her bottom lip in a nervous gesture he recognized and Gabe knew how worried she was. Guilt threatened again and was ruthlessly squashed. Hell, he wasn't hurting her. He was just giving her a hard time for a few days. Soon enough, she'd be back to her life and he'd have had the revenge he was due.

Watching her, as she stood so closely and yet so far from him, it finally came to Gabe just how to exact the payback his pride demanded. He was going to seduce her. Make her want him as he had once so desperately wanted her. And when she was limp with desire, ready to beg him to take her back…he'd cut her loose as surgically as she had done to him so long ago.

If that meant he would be forced to hold her captive on the island for a while longer, then that's just what he'd do. As he'd already told her…he owned the island and everything on it. Here, *he* made the rules.

"I called my friend Janine," she was saying, "and she said she'd get her fiancé to look into this for me, but I don't know what Max can do."

"Max?" he asked.

"Max Striver. He's—"

"I know Max," Gabe interrupted, and wondered if his old friend really had taken the plunge and proposed to the cute little brunette he'd spent so much time with in the last few weeks.

"You know him?"

"For a few years. And I never would have thought he'd get married again. Are you sure about this?"

"Hmm? What? Oh, yeah. Apparently he followed Janine home to Long Beach and proposed. They're getting married in London in a few weeks."

"Amazing," he mused, sitting on the corner of his desk. Of course, looking back, he could see that Max had been drawn deeper and deeper into the relationship with the woman he'd been paying to pretend to be his wife. Strange that now she'd be his wife for real. "He always said he'd never marry again."

"People change," she said lightly.

"Apparently." He shouldn't have been so surprised, really. He'd known that Max's father had been after him to marry and start building on the family dynasty.

Debbie was staring at him, a question in her eyes. "You never got married?"

"No." He stiffened, then forced himself to release the swift punch of tension gripping him. He hadn't thought of marriage again until recently. But that wasn't part of this conversation.

"Gabe…"

"Forget it," he said, not wanting to hear her explanation of why she'd turned down his marriage proposal ten years ago. It was over. And now, his life was different. *He* was different. He wasn't an eager young man following his heart anymore. Now he made decisions based on logic. Cool, clear logic.

"We should talk about it," she said. "About what happened between us."

"No point," he said. "It's over and done. Let it go. I have."

Four

Gabe insisted they have a late dinner at Fantasies' rooftop restaurant.

Debbie wanted to be doing *something* about her predicament, but since Gabe said all that could be done was being done, she'd had little choice but to try to relax. She wore the strapless, short black dress she'd brought with her on vacation, because it was the only dressy thing she had. But she also loved the way it fit, smoothing over her curves and flaring into a swirling skirt three inches above her knees.

Gabe's green eyes had fired when he first saw her in it and that little jolt of confidence had done a lot for her.

Now, they sat at a private table, on the corner of the roof, with a wide, black sky glittering with stars above them. The moon's reflection danced on the surface of the ocean and a soft breeze twisted the candle flames into a frenzied dance. The table was spread with a pristine, white-linen tablecloth and sported a single red rosebud in a crystal vase as a centerpiece. While the other people at the restaurant chatted and laughed, Debbie watched Gabe and wondered how he'd come so far in only ten years.

Physically, he looked much the same—long, thick, dark-blond hair, streaked gold now by the sun, a tall, lanky body that belied the strength in him. His face was sharp angles, piercing green eyes and a mouth that had, long ago, been able to reduce her to whimpers in seconds.

When she had known him, he'd been mostly a jeans and T-shirt kind of guy. Yet tonight, he wore a finely tailored tuxedo and looked as though he'd been born to it. In fact, with that long hair, pulled back at the nape of his neck, his high cheekbones and steady eyes, he looked both elegant and dangerous.

Enough to bring most women to their knees.

And she, Debbie thought, was no exception.

There was an air of tightly leashed power about him now that he hadn't had ten years ago. She'd noticed how the staff at Fantasies practically came to attention when he entered a room. He seemed to know every employee by name and every one of those employees jumped into action when he quirked a finger.

And she wondered again if there were some remnants of the man she'd once known beneath the veneer of sophistication he carried now.

"What're you thinking?" he asked, and she just barely caught the low rumble of his voice over the hum of conversations surrounding them.

Debbie smiled, reached for the glass of chilled white wine in front of her and took a sip to ease the dryness in her throat. "Just that you've changed a lot."

There was no answering smile in his eyes, but he nodded his head in acknowledgment. "I had plans. I saw to it that they succeeded."

If there was a barb in that statement, Debbie chose to ignore it. After all, ten years was a long time. Maybe he really had let the past go. Shouldn't she do the same? "I don't understand, though, how you did it? How'd you accomplish so much so quickly?"

He shifted his gaze to a nearby waiter, subtly signaled and had the man bustling over to top off their wineglasses. When the waiter had retreated again, Gabe said, "A combination of hard work and luck."

"I'm guessing that's the short version."

Briefly, his mouth curved into a half smile. "It is."

"How about the other version?"

He took a breath, blew it out and said, "There were a couple of lean years. Took a job in the Middle East, working security for the oil fields. Big money, not a lot of places to spend it." One shoulder lifted in a shrug. "I banked my pay, invested most of it."

Debbie lifted her wine again. "You can't tell me you did all this on simple investments."

"Hardly." He lifted his own wineglass, studied the straw-colored wine as it was backlit by the flickering candles and continued as if he were talking to himself rather than to her. He took a sip, set the glass down and leaned back in his chair.

"Several years ago, I met a guy who had an idea for some computer thing." He smiled ruefully and shook his head. "Didn't understand then what it was all about, still don't, really. But he seemed to know his stuff. He needed backing, I took a shot on him and hit the jackpot."

He told the story so simply, but she could see him in her mind's eye. Working in the Middle East, saving his money, investing it, taking a chance on another man with a dream. And finally, making all of his plans come true. A swell of admiration filled her as she remembered all the nights they'd spent talking about their dreams, their hopes.

He'd done everything he'd once talked about.

Accomplished so much.

"And then you bought the island?"

He let his gaze sweep the crowded rooftop restaurant before looking back at her. Pride shone in his eyes as he said, "Yes. I redid the hotel, renamed it and opened for business five years ago."

"It's a beautiful place," she said, and wished she didn't feel as though she were talking to a stranger. "You've really made something here, Gabe. Something people all over the world talk about."

The waiter approached again, served their meals, then dissolved into the background as silently as he'd arrived.

"What about you?" Gabe asked as she picked up a fork and lifted a bite of her pan-seared halibut. "What've you been doing since I last saw you?"

She chewed, swallowed and said, "I still live in Long Beach. I own a travel agency there."

"So you've done well."

Nodding, Debbie let her pride in her business fill her. True, she hadn't succeeded on the grand scale that Gabe had, but she'd made a good life for herself. One that was safe. Secure. And that was all that mattered to her. "Do you ever get back home?"

"No," he said, biting off the single word. "I left Long Beach ten years ago—"

He broke off and Debbie winced. She knew when he'd left. After their last night together, when she'd turned down his proposal. She'd tried to see him a few days later. To try to explain. To make him understand that it wasn't because she didn't love him.

But he'd already left and even his younger brother hadn't known where he'd gone. At least, Devlin Vaughn hadn't wanted to tell her.

"I went to your house," she said, wanting him to know that she hadn't simply turned her back on what they'd had. "But Devlin told me you were gone."

"No reason to stick around, was there?" He sliced off a piece of his swordfish and ate it. Then he gave her a small smile. "Don't look so guilty, Deb. You did what you had to do. So did I."

True, she had. She'd wanted to be with him, but her own fears hadn't allowed that choice. If her heart still hurt for chances missed and roads not taken, that was something she'd simply learned to live with.

But her throat was tight and swallowing wasn't easy.

So she forgot about dinner for the moment and had another sip of wine. "Well then, tell me what Dev's up to. Is he here working for you?"

"No, Dev runs his own businesses. He went into the military not long after I left. When he got out, he started a security firm—Top Dog. He keeps a team here on the island to work for the celebrity guests, but he's based out of L.A." Now his smile was genuine and even Debbie could see that the Vaughn brothers were as tight as they'd always been.

"Say hi to him for me when you see him next." Her fingers tapped restlessly on the tabletop as nerves jittered through her system. Didn't seem to matter that she kept trying to relax. Her body simply wouldn't allow it.

"Sure. Look." He leaned across the table again and reached out to lay one hand over her dancing fingers. "I know you're worried about the situation, but you're just gonna have to trust me. You couldn't do it ten years ago. Try harder now."

She frowned at him. "Gabe, I'm *trapped* here. Hard not to be a little on the anxious side."

"Trapped?" he repeated.

"I can't leave, can I?"

"No."

"Then…" She pulled her hand out from under his, picked up a braised carrot and took a small bite.

The candle flames threw dancing shadows across his face and his green eyes caught with the tiny fire. "I'll do what I can to help. I already told you that. And there are worse places to be stuck."

"I know that, it's just—"

"You never could stand not being in control," he mused, and eased back in his chair.

"So much for not talking about the past, then," Debbie pointed out.

He tipped his head. "You always were stubborn, Debbie. Determined to have things your own way."

"So were you." She waved one arm, encompassing their lush surroundings. "You built a world just the way you wanted it to be. How is that any different from me?"

"Suppose it's not," he agreed. "But in this case, what you want has to wait on a few other factors."

She dropped her fork and it clinked musically against the fine china. "No one is really going to believe I'm the jewel thief, are they?"

He shrugged negligently, as if it didn't matter to him one way or the other. "The authorities have to check it out."

"And how long is that going to take?"

"Things move a little slower in the islands."

"Fabulous."

He laughed shortly. "I can promise to be an understanding jailer."

Debbie looked across the table at him and wished she could see into his thoughts. His smile was cool, pleasant, but his eyes held secrets and that bothered her more than she cared to admit. Just the night before he hadn't seemed so eager to make her happy. Hadn't he said something like, *I own everything on this island, including you?* So what happened to change his attitude?

"Something wrong?"

"You tell me," she said, pushing her plate away since clearly she wasn't going to be able to swallow anything beyond her wine. "Why're you being so nice all of a sudden?"

He reached up, loosened the tie at his neck and then undid the top button of his dress shirt. Instead of making him look more relaxed, it only served to make him appear edgier. Sexier, God help her. Her palms went damp and her mouth went dry.

His eyes glittered and his features stiffened. "Maybe I just don't see any point in being enemies."

She wanted to believe him. She wished she could. "Really?"

"Really." Gabe looked at her for a long, silent minute. He heard the hope in her voice, saw the vulnerability in her eyes. And he knew this was going according to plan. She was trusting him. Of course, what choice did she have?

She watched him and his gaze slid over her in appreciation. His body reacted in an instant. She was beautiful. Enough to take a man's breath. She was made for moonlight. Her skin seemed to glow, her eyes shone and her mouth…

He pulled in a breath, reminded himself that this was just a ploy. He was here to lower *her* guard, not his own. He was being nice, as she put it, with that single goal in mind. And he was a man who never gave up once his course was set.

He wanted her.

Hell, he'd always wanted her. From the very first time he'd laid eyes on her. She'd been only eighteen years old, and his blood had pumped and his brain had dissolved. She had been the one sure thing in his life.

Until she'd walked away.

Now, he had her right where he wanted her. And he was going to seduce her into thinking all was forgiven. He was going to make her want him as she once had. And then when he'd had her under him, over him, every way he could think of, he'd be the one to walk away.

With that thought in mind, he took a sip of wine, arrowed his gaze into hers and said, "So you never got married, either, huh?"

She blinked. "Wow. There's a change of subject."

He shrugged. "Just a question."

"Right. Okay." Nodding, she sipped at her own wine and said, "No, I never married. I was engaged earlier this year, though."

Something inside him fisted. He didn't like how it affected him to know that she had found a man she loved enough to say yes to. A man she apparently had loved far more than she had him. Strange that after all this time, he would even care. But there it was. "So you managed to say yes to a proposal, after all."

She flushed and shot him a quick look. "Gabe."

He shook his head, forced himself to smile. "But even after saying yes, you backed out. Haven't changed much, have you, Deb?"

"I didn't back out."

"Really? So where's your husband?" Gabe looked past her at the crowd as if searching for a particular face before shifting his gaze back to hers.

"I said *I* didn't back out."

"Ah," he smiled then, "so he turned the tables on you, did he?"

"No." Scowling now, she blew out a breath and said, "It just didn't happen."

"Why not?"

He watched her, saw emotions churning in her eyes and couldn't identify any of them. There had once been a time, he thought, that he knew what she was thinking. That they were so connected, they could have completed each other's sentences. But that time was long gone.

She shifted uncomfortably in her chair. Her fingers swept up and down the stem of her wineglass and her mouth firmed fiercely as if she were biting back words that battled to get free. Finally, though, she met his gaze and said quietly, "I found out that Mike was already married. To two other women."

"Ah…" Despite the fury trembling in her voice, he heard the pain, too, the humiliation, and a small part of him was glad of it. Why should he be the only one to remember how it felt to have someone you loved pull the rug out from under you? Besides, he wasn't here to sympathize. "So you chose badly, *again.*"

She took another sip of wine. "All those years ago, Gabe," she said, "we were too young."

"I loved you."

"And I loved you."

"Not enough."

"You're wrong," she said. "But love isn't everything."

Now she reached across the table toward him, but Gabe pulled his hand back.

He resented her bringing their shared past back to gnaw at him. For years, Gabe had deliberately kept those memories in lockdown, refusing to think about them, refusing to wallow in what he had concluded had been a mistake, right from the beginning. The past had no part in his life. His present was just as he wanted it and his future was planned out.

And she wasn't a part of it.

Yet, just by being here, she was neatly undoing all of those carefully arranged locks he'd put in place. But damn, if he was going to make it easy on her.

"We keep heading down that road and I'm just not interested in the past, Deb. It was a long time ago and we're different people now. You said it yourself. People change." He stood and shoved both hands into the pockets of his tux. Looking down at her, he said, "Stay. Enjoy your dinner. I've got some things to look into."

"Gabe, don't go."

The softness in her voice pulled at him. The yearning in her eyes tugged at something deep inside. He didn't want to be tugged, but no way would he be the one to bend in this little contest.

He lifted one hand to her face, stroked his fingertips along the soft, smooth line of her jaw and said, "I'll see you later."

* * *

"You want me to *what?*"

Gabe leaned back in his desk chair and looked up at his head of security. Yes, his brother, Devlin, kept a team of private security on the island, but this man, Victor Reyes, worked for Gabe. Victor had been in charge of island security for four years now and in that time, he and Gabe had become friends.

"I want you to make sure Debbie Harris knows she's being watched."

Victor was a tall, muscular man with a fierce expression, forbidding personality and black, glittering eyes. It was usually enough for him to simply show up and anyone causing trouble at Fantasies was quickly convinced to change their mind. "Can I ask why?"

"She thinks she's under suspicion of being the jewel thief wanted on the islands."

Victor's eyes narrowed. "You have reason to believe she's the thief?"

"No." Gabe got up and turned to face the wide bank of windows behind his desk. "She's not a thief. But I'm not ready for her to leave the island just yet and I'm willing to do what I have to do to keep her here."

There was a long moment of silence and Gabe knew that Victor was considering his next words before he spoke. A careful man. "I guess you've got your reasons."

"Yeah, I do."

"All right, then," Victor said. "You're the boss."

Gabe glanced over his shoulder at the other man. "But you don't think it's a good idea."

"You don't pay me to think, Gabe," Victor said, folding massive arms across his chest. "But if you want my opinion, no. It's not the best idea you've ever had."

Probably not, Gabe thought, turning back to stare out at the spread of the world he'd built stretching in front of him. Would have been smarter to let Debbie go never knowing he was on the island. But this felt right. He'd learned long ago to listen to his instincts, so he was going to go with that. There was a score to be settled between him and Debbie Harris.

Turning around, Gabe faced his old friend and nodded. "You're probably right, Vic. But we're gonna do this my way."

"Okay by me. But what're you going to do about Ms. Madison?"

"Huh?" Gabe felt the world tip slightly, but looked at his friend and asked, "What're you talking about? What's Grace got to do with this?"

Victor shook his head and pulled a PalmPilot from the pocket of the lightweight jacket he wore to cover up the gun at his hip. Turning the device on, he scanned the screen, looked up at Gabe and said, "According to the schedule, Ms. Madison's due to arrive in three days."

"Damn it."

How could he have forgotten this? Grace's visit had been arranged more than a month ago. But then, in the last month, he hadn't thought about much more than Debbie Harris. Hardly surprising he'd forget about other plans when he was so wrapped up in his scheme for revenge.

Muttering dark threats just under his breath, Gabe shoved one hand through his hair, then kicked the edge of his desk. "I forgot all about her."

Victor chuckled and put his PalmPilot away.

"This amuses you?" Gabe asked, his voice a thin, cold ribbon.

Victor wasn't cowed, though. They'd been friends too long. He simply smiled and said, "You've got Debbie Harris staying in your suite…and in three days, your *fiancée* shows up. What's not amusing about that?"

Gabe scowled at him. Grace wasn't his fiancée. Not officially. He hadn't proposed, though he and Grace had reached an agreement the last time she'd visited. *Debbie.* Without even trying, she was messing with his life. "We're not engaged. Yet."

"Oh, well, then. No problem."

Gabe slumped back into his desk chair. Disgusted, he glanced at his friend. "You're fired."

"Hell, boss, you can't fire me. I'm the only friend you've got left."

Five

Gabe had come a long way from Long Beach, CA. Mingling with the rich, the powerful, the famous, he was completely at home. He wore a tuxedo as though he'd been born to it and used a smooth, practiced charm on the "beautiful" people surrounding him. And while he looked relaxed, Debbie could see, even at a distance, that his gaze was sharp as he swept the room, making sure everything was as it should be.

Then a glamorous brunette in a fire-engine-red dress that dipped low over her huge, had-to-be-man-made breasts and ended high on her thighs, leaned into Gabe and whispered something in his ear. He gave her a slow smile that set off a bubble of something hot and ugly in the pit of Debbie's stomach. She didn't have the right, of course, to care that he was smiling at a woman who clearly didn't know the meaning of the word "subtle."

But that didn't seem to matter. When the brunette dipped her head and looked up at him through her lashes, Debbie muttered, "Oh, for God's sake. What is this, Seduction 101?"

At least Gabe wasn't buying what the woman seemed so intent on selling. He smiled again, then turned his attention back to the older, sophisticated couple standing on his right. The brunette pouted for a minute, then slipped into the crowd.

"Happy hunting," Debbie whispered as she watched the scene play out from the doorway of Fantasies' main club. A swirl of nerves jittered through her stomach and had her taking a long, deep breath in a futile attempt to settle herself.

Gabe may completely be at ease here, but she felt as out of place as a discount store in Beverly Hills. She knew she was here under false pretenses. After all, the people crowding this club were wealthy, pampered. She owned and operated a travel agency in Long Beach. She couldn't be more different from Fantasies' usual guests.

Nerves rattled through her again and she tried to ignore them. DJ-driven music pumped through cleverly disguised speakers on the dark-red walls and candlelight waved and flickered on every tabletop. On the dance floor, couples swayed in sensuous patterns, conversations and laughter rose and fell like waves on the ocean, and amid the sea of people, Debbie felt suddenly alone.

The only person she knew here was Gabe, and he was more or less a stranger now, anyway. Ten years was a long time and what they'd had together then had nothing to do with today.

Her hair was swept up into a tangle of curls and the soft kiss of an air-conditioned breeze brushed the back of Debbie's neck. She shivered a bit, but knew it had little to do with the cool air and more to do with the uneasy situation she found herself in—depending on a man who had no reason to think well of her and no way of getting back home.

"Deep thoughts?"

Gabe's voice rumbled across her nerve endings and she jolted a little as she turned to find him standing right beside her. His green eyes shone with an emotion she couldn't quite identify and the subtle, spicy scent of his aftershave seemed to reach out for her. The man was a walking hormone assault.

"I didn't hear you come up."

"Looked like you were too busy thinking to hear much of anything."

"I guess so," she admitted, keeping her gaze locked with his.

When he smiled, the secrets in his eyes shifted, softened. Then he held one hand out to her and as she took it he said, "You look beautiful."

The deep, sapphire-blue dress fit snug to her curves, as if it had been designed especially for her. It snaked down her hips and belled around her knees to fall to the floor in a fluid sweep of silky fabric. She'd never owned such an amazing dress and still wasn't sure she should have accepted it.

She'd found it laid out for her on Gabe's bed—and the shoes and matching bag were alongside it. Logically, she knew that buying her this dress had been no more to him than picking up a quart of milk at the corner grocery. But illogically, she felt wrong wearing a dress given to her by a man who didn't even like her.

Swallowing hard, she said, "Thank you for the dress, Gabe. Really. It's beautiful. But—"

"If you're about to tell me I didn't have to do it, save your breath." He tucked her hand through the crook of his arm and led her into the crowded club. "I wanted you here tonight and you needed something appropriate."

Meaning nothing she'd brought with her would do. Well, hard to be insulted by the truth. But still, it irritated her to have to acknowledge it.

"Thanks, anyway."

"You're welcome." He looked down at her, smiled again and Debbie's knees went a little wobbly.

A simple hormonal reaction, she assured herself as he steered her toward the dance floor. Didn't mean a thing. Then he pulled her into the circle of his arms and slid into the crowd of slowly moving people on the gleaming wood floor.

His arms felt good—right. She moved against him and memories crowded her mind. Memories of a slow dance with him on the Long Beach pier one cold, autumn night ten years ago. The moon had been out, casting shadows over them and the dozen or so people joining them on the pier.

The scent of the sea had whipped around their bodies, the sweet rush of love had flowed between them. He'd smiled at her then, just as he was now, and when he'd kissed her, she'd known she loved him.

"You're thinking again," he whispered, bending his head to hers so that his voice and his breath caressed her ear, sending another shiver over her body.

"Just…remembering," she said, her hand on his shoulder tightening, to help her balance.

"The pier."

Her head tipped back and she stared up at him, surprised somehow, that he'd allowed himself that memory. Hadn't he made a point in the last couple of days, of telling her that he had no interest in the past?

"You remember?"

He moved her into a slow turn, his arm about her waist squeezed, pulling her closer to him. Close enough that she felt the hard ridge of his body pressing into hers.

"Just because I don't want to think about the past doesn't mean I've lost the memories."

"They're good memories," she said, and watched sadly as the shutters dropped over his eyes again. He was still here, with her, but his emotions had closed down, shutting her out, shutting out anything that might have been warming between them. And something inside her was sorry for it.

He stared at her, his gaze moving over her face with the sureness of a touch. "Not all of them."

"No," she admitted, hardly noticing the blur of motion from the dancers moving past them. They were nothing more than a wash of brilliant colors, blending together into a swirl of distraction. "But most of them are good, Gabe. Do we have to lose it all because of the way it ended?"

"I found out a long time ago that it's better that way. Cleaner."

His arm still held her close, belying the distance in his words. "But emptier."

"The present's full enough for me," he countered.

"Is it?" She tore her gaze from his long enough to look around the crowded club, to take in some of what he'd built before meeting his gaze again. "You fill it with people like the brunette in the red dress and that's all you need?"

His mouth quirked. "You jealous of the brunette?"

"Oh, please." Irritation spiked because, yes, she *had* been jealous, even if it hadn't lasted long. "If those boobs are real, I'll eat my pretty new dress."

He laughed out loud and the sound of it rolled over the music and settled over her like a blessing from the past. God, she'd loved the sound of his laughter. And his smile had always been enough to light up every corner of her heart. How could she have forgotten? Self-preservation, that's how, she reminded herself. If she'd spent the last ten years remembering what she'd given up, she'd never have been able to be happy.

"Ashley Strong is a very nice woman."

Debbie gasped and looked past his shoulder as if she could spot the woman. "That was Ashley Strong? The actress?"

"You didn't recognize her?"

"No." And she didn't see her now. Debbie'd been too busy being sickened by the woman's blatant attempt at seduction to pay much attention to who she might be. She looked up at Gabe. "But now I know for *sure* those boobs aren't hers."

He laughed again and swept her into a wide turn, his hand firmly on the small of her back. "Damned if I haven't missed that smart mouth of yours, Deb."

"You missed me?"

His smile faded and the shutter over his eyes snapped into place. "For a while, I missed you with every breath I took. But it's different now."

"Maybe," she said, and held on to his shoulder tightly. "You say your present's very full. Yet I watch you working the crowd, Gabe, and I see you surrounded by all of these people, but you're not actually connected to any of them."

One corner of his mouth quirked. "How do you know?"

"Because I know you. You're here, but you keep yourself separate from everyone else. I can see it in your eyes."

He frowned at her now and the arm around her waist eased off just a little. "You used to know me, I grant you that. But it's been a long time, Deb. I'm not the man you knew. You should trust me on that."

The music ended and without another word he guided her across the floor to the owner's table, set in the shadows along the far wall and closed off from the rest of the guests. She slid in, then watched him as he took his place beside her. There was an open bottle of champagne chilling in a silver ice bucket waiting for them. Gabe reached for it, filled two crystal flutes and handed one of them to her.

"So what do you say, you let go of the past and take me as I am today."

"I thought I was."

"Not really." He turned the flute in his long fingers, stroking the fragile crystal stem with concentration enough to make Debbie remember how it had felt to have those fingers moving over her skin. His gaze turned to hers. "You see me, but you also see the shadow of a man who once loved you."

Those words jabbed at her insides like thorns pricking her skin.

"I'm not that man anymore."

"I know that."

"I wonder."

She took a sip of champagne, letting the icy froth caress her dry throat. Around them, the club patrons partied, oblivious to the whispered conversation flowing in the shadows.

"Oh, I know you're not *that* Gabe." Debbie looked at him and said, "If you were the man I remember, you would have been doing more to help me out of this mess."

He eased back against the red-leather banquette. Lifting one arm to drape along the back of the booth, he turned in his seat to face her completely. His features were smooth, even, betraying nothing of what he was feeling. "I told you it would take a few days."

"You haven't heard anything new?"

He paused, took a drink of champagne, then shook his head. "Nothing."

"And you haven't tried."

"Are you under the impression I'm trying to keep you here?" he asked.

"I'm not sure," Debbie admitted. "But I know there's more going on than you're telling me."

"You've a suspicious mind," he quipped. "Strange, I don't remember that about you."

"And that's not really an answer," Debbie countered, tipping her head to one side to study the elegant, sexy man sitting so close to her. "You talk, but you don't really say anything. I don't remember you being so…flexible."

He laughed shortly, set his glass down and leaned in toward her. His eyes became the world. Those deep, green eyes that had once captivated her, that had once held all of the world she'd ever wanted.

"What do you want from me, Deb?"

"Your help."

"You've got that," he said easily, letting his gaze sweep briefly to the swell of her breasts. "Anything else?"

Her mouth watered and a flicker of heat licked at her insides. There was too much she wanted and couldn't have. Mostly, she thought, *him*. She wanted him every bit as much as she once had. "Gabe…"

He reached for her hand and smoothed his thumb across her palm. She shivered, closed her eyes and hissed in a shaky breath.

"This isn't about the past, Debbie," he said. "This is about now. About tonight. About us and what we could share together."

Tempting. So tempting. To forget about all the worries niggling at her. To forget that she was trapped by losing herself in Gabe.

"You're thinking again," he said, a small smile curving his lips.

"And I shouldn't?"

He lifted her hand to his mouth, kissed the palm, nibbled at her skin and Debbie felt herself melting. Heat swamped her, need crashed through her and her brain short-circuited. If he'd been trying to keep her from thinking, he was doing a good job.

Sliding toward her on the booth seat, he pulled her close, wrapped one arm around her and looked into her eyes as he said, "Sometimes, it's better to just shut down your mind and let your body take over."

God knew, his own body was more than ready. Since the moment he'd seen her again, he'd wanted her. And now, as Victor had reminded him only that afternoon, Gabe was running out of time. Soon enough, he'd have to let her go. But not before he'd had her again. Made her regret ever walking away from him.

Her blue eyes were wide and easily read. There was passion and confusion and enough desire to turn the burning embers inside him into an inferno. Gabe stroked his fingertips along the nape of her neck and felt the tremors that rocked her move through him, too.

Just touching her inflamed him. She was the only

woman he'd ever known who could make his body hard with a look. His plan to seduce her and then discard her was suddenly taking on a life of its own. He wanted her now more than he ever had. Ten years ago, he'd had her for his own and lost her.

Tonight, he would reclaim her.

"Stop thinking, Deb," he whispered, and bent his head to kiss the curve of her neck. She shivered, and sighed a little, the tiny sound slipping inside him.

The taste of her filled him. The scent of her surrounded him. And there in the shadows, he felt a surge of need he'd never known before. Pulling her in closer, he wrapped his arms around her, lifted his head long enough to look down into her eyes. Then slowly, he lowered his mouth to hers. One brush of his lips across hers and her breath puffed out on a half sigh.

"Gabe…"

"Shh…" He slid his left hand down her rib cage, following the line of her body, feeling her breath shudder in and out of her lungs. She went limp in his grasp as she leaned into him and Gabe knew he had her. Knew that she wanted him as much as he needed her.

His mouth claimed hers. He used his tongue to part her lips and at the first taste of her, he felt the years roll back. And the crowded club became a lonely beach in California. She moved into him and her body fit with his as well as it ever had. As if they'd been made for each other, two pieces of the same puzzle. Two halves of the same whole.

And yet, even as those thoughts rushed through his

mind, Gabe forced them away. This wasn't about kismet. Fate. Love. This was about revenge, pure and simple.

He wanted her gasping, writhing beneath him. He wanted her hot and needy, and when he took her to the precipice and over, he wanted her trembling for more. Only then would he be able to walk away, knowing that *she* would be the haunted one now. Knowing that she would spend the next ten years thinking about him, wondering what might have been.

She tore her mouth from his. "Gabe, I—"

"No thinking," he reminded her, sliding his left hand up now to cup her breast. Her nipple was hard, pressing against the cool silk fabric and responding to his touch eagerly. His thumb and forefinger tweaked and pulled at the so-tender bud of flesh and Debbie twisted in his grasp. Her eyes closed on another sigh as she moved into him, losing herself in the shadows. Giving herself up to his touch.

"That feels…"

"Amazing," he finished for her, then took her mouth again, this time with more need than tenderness. With more hunger than care. He needed, so he took. He wanted, so he claimed. His tongue clashed with hers, his breath mingled with hers. Her sighs became his as he devoured her, taking all she offered and demanding more.

He slipped his left hand beneath the bodice of her dress to cup her bare breast in the palm of his hand. He kneaded her flesh, tugging at her nipple until she groaned into his mouth and arched into him.

Shadows danced around them, fed by the candle-light, softened by the whirl of bodies on the dance floor. There was a partition, separating his table from the rest of the club, but Gabe knew it wasn't enough. The crush of the crowd was only a few feet away.

For what he wanted from Debbie, he required privacy. He needed her naked and moving beneath him. Her hand cupped his cheek as he kissed her and the simple feel of her hand on his face fired his blood and brought an ache he hadn't known in years to the corners of his heart.

At that stray thought, he instantly pulled back from her. He didn't want his heart touched. He wasn't looking for affection. *For love.* All he wanted from her was the physical. The slide of her body over his. The taste of her flesh in his mouth. The sound of her sighs in his ears.

"Gabe," she said a little breathlessly, "is everything all right?"

"Fine," he lied. "But we need to get out of here."

She licked her lips and his gaze fixed on that simple, innocent action. His body tightened and his blood rushed through his veins.

"Yes," she said. "Let's go. Now."

Just what he wanted to hear.

Sliding from the booth, he held out one hand to her and when she slipped her hand into his, he tightened his grip and tugged her to his side. He hooked his right arm around her waist and held her close as they started through the crowded club.

He led her through the mass of people, threading his

way with a single-minded determination that had stood him in good stead over the past ten years. He knew what he wanted and how to get it, and never let anything get in his way.

Tonight was no different.

He told himself the rush of expectation filling him was no more than the knowledge that he was about to get his revenge on her. And he was sticking to that story.

When they were free of the club and headed across the lobby to the bank of elevators, the concierge called out to him. Gabe waved him off, tucked Debbie even closer to him and hurried his pace.

"I feel like I can't breathe."

He glanced down at her, saw the shine in her eyes and the high flush on her cheeks and nearly kissed her. But once he started kissing her again, he wouldn't stop. His fingers pressed into her side, sneaking up to stroke the side of her breast. She groaned quietly, bit her bottom lip and gave him a shaky smile.

"I know just how you feel," he said, and quickened his pace even further. The heels of their shoes clicked rhythmically against the tile floor and sounded, to Gabe's fevered brain, like a clock ticking off the seconds until he could have her naked and panting beneath him.

Past the bank of guest elevators was the private car that went directly to the owner's suite. Gabe pulled his key card from his breast pocket, swept it through the reader and then pulled Debbie into the elevator as soon as the doors parted for them.

When the door swept quietly closed and the elevator began its climb, Debbie moved into his arms. He pulled her in tightly to him, wrapping his arms around her middle and holding on as if the touch of her meant life.

She moved against him and he remembered vividly, wildly, how out of control and frenzied their lovemaking had always been. He'd never found that passion with anyone else. Never known again the flashing heat of desire that overpowered all of a man's senses at once.

With Debbie there was heat, fire, explosive need. She slid her hands beneath his tuxedo jacket and ran her palms over his shirtfront. Even through the fine linen fabric, he felt the sizzle of her skin on his and relished the flames, knowing that she was burning for him. Knowing that she was feeling exactly what he wanted her to feel. He walked her backward until she hit the wall, and took her mouth with his in a fierce kiss that demanded and gave and demanded again.

Her breath puffed against his cheek. She leaned into him, arching her hips into his as if looking for the release that was so very close.

He tore his mouth from hers, tasted the line of her throat and felt her pulse pounding erratically. He had her. Had her hungry for him, wild for him.

What he hadn't counted on, though, was his own need. His own desire nearly swamping him. He had counted on the fact that he could reach her as he once had. But he'd never expected to feel any stirrings himself. He'd thought only to have her, ease his body's ache and make her whimper for him.

But there was more going on here. There was more pushing through him and he didn't like it—didn't want to admit it, despite the clamoring of his own blood and the hammering pound of his heartbeat.

No, he told himself. He was in this for one reason. Payback.

"Now, Deb. Right here, right now." He couldn't wait any longer.

She looked into his eyes and whispered, "Yes, Gabe. Right now. Please, right now."

He reached down, gathered up the hem of her sapphire-blue gown and lifted it, sliding his hand along her leg, higher, higher. She trembled, spread her legs farther apart in silent invitation and when he cupped her heat, he felt a jolt of surprise.

"No panties?" One eyebrow lifted as he cupped his hand over her again.

She gasped, then smiled and shrugged. "Panty lines."

"Let's hear it for tight gowns," he said, and stroked the hard bud of her sex while she cried his name.

Six

Debbie's brain shrieked, *Mistake!! Stop now!!*

But her body so didn't want to hear it. This is what she'd been headed for since the moment she first saw Gabe at the tiny island jail. The passion between them was as rich and thick as it ever had been. Clearly, ten years apart had done nothing to lessen it.

His hands on her body felt like fire. His fingertips seared her skin and when he dipped one finger inside her, Debbie's body roared into life.

She gasped, arched into him and tipped her head back, staring blindly at the ceiling of the elevator car. Her hips rocked into his touch. Rational thought dribbled away. His mouth at the curve of her neck fed the heat pulsing inside her and when his thumb flicked over the core of her, she shuddered in his grasp. Instantly a quick, greedy climax erupted, threatening to swamp her.

"Good," he whispered, his voice muffled against her skin. "Now again."

"Can't." She choked out the single word as the last of her tremors eased away. Shaking her head, she looked at him and whispered, "I can't. It's too much. Too fast. Too soon."

"It's never enough." His gaze locked on hers and she fell into the green depths. "I want to watch you go over. I want to feel you shake for me."

His thumb stroked her again and she whimpered as a pleasure/pain jolted across her too-sensitive flesh.

The elevator doors dinged and opened into his living room. The wood floors gleamed in the lamplight, the bright rugs scattered over the floor shone like gemstones tossed to the ground. He set her on her feet, but her knees were like jelly.

Instantly he swept her up into his arms and Debbie hooked her own arms around his neck. Burrowing into him, she tucked her head against his chest and listened to the wild crashing of his heartbeat.

His long, hurried steps took them through the living room without a pause and when they entered the master bedroom, he didn't waste any time. He stretched her out on the bed, but when she reached for him, lifting her arms to him in welcome, he held her wrists and slowly turned her around. She felt his fingers at her back and when he pulled down the zipper of her dress, the cool air caressed her heated skin like a promise.

"Gorgeous," he murmured, and bent to kiss her at the small of her back. She sighed and closed her eyes as his lips touched her in an intimate touch. Then as he pulled her gown off, his hands cupped her behind, his fingers squeezing, kneading.

Debbie groaned and twisted on the silken duvet, the cool slide of the fabric adding to the sensation overload slapping her system.

She burned for him all over again. It was as if her body hadn't shattered at all just a few minutes ago. She ached to be taken again. Ached to feel his body invading hers. His lean but muscled body crushing down on her. "Gabe…"

"Right here, babe," he murmured the words as he trailed nibbling kisses up and down the length of her spine. While his mouth teased her, his hands explored her. Dipping into every curve, exploring every inch of her body until Debbie could hardly breathe with the fire caging her lungs.

"I want…" *You,* she thought. *You.* She needed him desperately. Wanted him even more. Her mind was a whirling jumble of racing thoughts that splintered when she tried to catch hold of them. But it didn't matter. She didn't need to think.

Only needed to feel.

Only needed *him.*

She tried to roll over so that she could see him, touch

him, do to him what he was doing to her. But he held
her in place with his strong hands.

"Not yet." He kissed the nape of her neck, scraping
his teeth against her skin and she groaned softly. "Just
let me touch you."

She buried her face in the silky duvet and curled her
hands into fists over the material, as if she needed a firm
grip on the world to keep from sliding off. She twisted
and writhed beneath him, her skin burning, itching for
him, and when his hands stopped their exploration, she
whimpered again and couldn't even blame herself for
the sighed complaint.

Looking back over her shoulder, she watched as he
quickly tore his clothing off and tossed it to the floor to
join her discarded gown. She licked her lips in anticipation as the pale, gold lamplight fell on his hard,
muscled chest, his flat abdomen, his... He was big.
Bigger even than she remembered. And obviously more
than ready for her.

Her core tingled in expectation. Her body trembled
with want. She rolled over to welcome him.

"Gabe...I need you. Now."

"I know," he said, and she saw a brief, half smile
curve his mouth. "And you're going to want me even
more in a minute."

He lifted her hips, and she wrapped her legs around
his waist in invitation. "Gabe..."

"Trust me," he whispered.

He stroked her behind, his fingers dancing over her
flesh as if he were coaxing a beautiful tune from a

concert piano. Debbie sighed and then gasped as his fingers dipped inside her again, exploring, stroking, goading her higher and higher on the climb to satisfaction.

Her hips rocked with the rhythm he set. Her breath hitched as he stroked her damp heat. She grabbed fistfuls of the duvet again as her hold on the world began to tumble from her grasp. And still, he pushed her higher.

"Please, Gabe…"

He shifted, the bed dipping with his movements. She blew out her breath, lifted her hips for him and sucked in a gulp of air when his body plunged into hers. The feel of him, thick and hard and eager, filled her. It was as if he was taking not only her body, but her soul. Pushing himself so high and deep within her that she couldn't breathe.

Couldn't imagine existing without him being a part of her.

His hands slid up and down her sides, scorching her skin with his heat. She sighed and moved against him, taking him deeper still, higher. She needed to feel all of him within her. Needed to fill the emptiness within.

She'd spent ten years denying what this man really had meant to her. Ten years where she'd talked herself into believing that the connection between them hadn't been as deep and all-consuming as she remembered. Ten years where she'd convinced herself that life without Gabe was just as good as life *with* Gabe.

She'd even lied to herself enough that she'd accepted a marriage proposal from a man who had never touched her heart as Gabe did without even trying.

And in that one crashing moment, she recognized the lies she'd told herself for what they really were. Cold comfort to take the edge off of what she had walked away from.

He moved within her, taking her, staking a claim, and Debbie gave herself up to the glory of it. She bit down on her lip to keep from crying out with the pleasure jolting through her and closed her eyes to hide the tears of completion welling there. He rocked against her, over and over again. She heard his heavy breathing, felt the tension coiled in him and reaching for her. Felt the amazing, soul-satisfying hum of their bodies moving as one and knew…finally *knew* that she loved him.

Desperately.

Eternally.

She loved Gabe Vaughn and nothing could change it. Not time. Not her own foolishness.

Nothing.

She moved eagerly, frantically, twisting against him, and heard him groan in reaction. That soft, helpless sound urged her on.

"Enough." The word came out on a strangled growl. He pulled his body free of hers and before she could complain, took a jagged breath and looked down into her eyes.

Green. Forest-green and filled with shadows, his gaze moved over her in a hot sweep that shook her right to her bones. Then, leaning to one side, he snatched open the drawer of a bedside table, grabbed up a condom and ripped the package open in a frenzy. He sheathed himself in a second and then loomed over her again, bracing himself on his hands, placed at either side of her head.

She stared up at him and saw the man she'd dreamed of for ten long years. She cupped his face between her palms and whispered, "Come to me, Gabe."

He didn't speak. Didn't have to. She read all she wanted to know in his eyes. The flash of hunger. The spark of something deeper. The gleam of need. It was all there.

Then he slid into her heat and Debbie nearly gasped. She held him deep within her. Reveled in the hard, solid weight of him atop her. Loved the feel of his body locked inside hers.

When he rocked his hips, pushing himself deeper, she gave herself up to the magic she'd only ever found with him. She matched his rhythm, moving with him in a dance that seemed as new as it did familiar. She ran her palms up and down his back, scoring his skin with her nails. She inhaled the scent of him and dropped a kiss at the base of his throat before meeting his mouth with hers.

His tongue pushed inside, tangled with hers and as they devoured each other, his body continued to plunge inside. Fiercely, passionately, he claimed her again and again, taking her higher, faster, than she'd ever been before.

The first twist of release spun out inside her and Debbie gasped, lifting her hips into his, tipping her head back on the bed, holding on to him as though he were her only remaining link to the world.

And then it was more.

It was everything.

Her body splintered and her mind shattered. She shouted his name, held him tightly and rode the wave of amazing sensation that carried her into oblivion. And when he called her name and followed her, Debbie was there, waiting to catch him as he fell.

Gabe rolled to one side of her and then pushed off the bed. He needed a little distance from Debbie. A little bit of room so that he could catch his breath and congratulate himself on a job well done.

After all, that's what this had been about. Seduction. Sex. Payback. It had worked like a charm, he told himself. He had her right where he wanted her. Glancing over his shoulder, he looked briefly at Debbie, stretched out across the duvet, practically purring in contentment.

And he wanted her again.

That hadn't been the plan, but plans were meant to be changed, right? Just because he'd had her once didn't mean the game was over. Until she left—until he let her go—she was his.

"That was…" Her voice trailed off as if she couldn't quite find the right descriptive words.

"Yeah." He knew how she felt. Damned if he could come up with a word to describe what that experience had been like, either. So he put it out of his head, forced his voice into a casual tone and said, "You want a drink? I want a drink."

He walked naked from the bedroom into the living

area and headed straight for the bar. Soft lamplight spilled across the room, chasing shadows into the corners. The sheer drapes across the open French doors lifted and danced in a whisper of a breeze that carried the scent of the ocean into the room.

At the bar, he opened the under-the-counter refrigerator and pulled out a bottle of Chardonnay. Debbie liked white wine, he knew, and it would do for him, as well. He opened the bottle and had the first glass poured before she strolled out of the bedroom wearing only his black bathrobe. He didn't want to think about her naked body beneath the silk fabric, so he swallowed hard and asked, "Wine?"

"Thanks," she said, and crossed barefoot to him to accept the glass.

Gabe tossed back his drink as if it were medicinal, then quickly poured another. He stared down into the gold liquid, willing himself to settle. It wasn't working. Blowing out a breath, he crossed the room and stepped through the fluttering curtains and out onto the terrace. Didn't matter here if he was naked or not. This was a private balcony and couldn't be seen from anywhere else on the island.

The cool ocean air caressed his skin and did a good job of banking the embers still warming inside him. How could he want her again so quickly?

"Aren't you cold?" She stepped up beside him, laid one hand on the stone railing and took a sip of her wine.

"No." He didn't want to talk to her. He didn't want to know what she was thinking and he sure as hell wasn't up to having one of those post-coital conversations all women seemed to thrive on. Damn it, what he *wanted* to do was to throw her down on the terrace and lose himself inside her again.

Lowering to admit that he was getting tangled up in his own damn trap.

"Gabe…"

He turned his head to look at her. The soft breeze ruffled her hair. Her eyes were shining and her mouth looked too damned delectable for safety. So he kept his voice tight, his tone grim as he said, "Don't start."

"Start what?"

He snorted, took a sip of wine. "You know what. Have sex with a woman and she wants to talk about the future, for God's sake."

She blinked at him, frowned and said, "I wasn't going to talk about the future at all."

"Fine," he snapped. "Then let's talk about the past."

Stupid, he thought. No reason to bring up what's long dead and buried. But when her mouth flattened into a grim line, he enjoyed it too much to stop. "You want to talk. So talk."

"What're you so pissed about?"

"Hell if I know," he muttered, taking another long drink of his wine.

"You know, you used to be in a *better* mood after sex," she said through gritted teeth.

"I *used* to do a lot of things differently." His gaze locked on hers and for several humming seconds, neither of them said a word.

"Unbelievable," she said quietly. "You can stand there and be all snotty and standoffish after what we just did together?"

"It was just sex."

"It was more than that," she countered.

"Not to me."

"Liar."

"You don't know me, Deb. Not anymore."

"You're wrong," she said and set her wineglass down on the stone railing. Lifting her chin, she stared up into his eyes and challenged him with a hot glare. "I *do* know you, Gabe. You haven't changed that much in ten years. And for some reason you're supremely pissed off—not at me. At yourself."

He choked out a laugh and looked away from those blue eyes because damned if they weren't seeing too much. Staring out at the moonlight scattering across the ocean's surface, he said, "Now you're a psychologist? Well, you're wasting your time analyzing me, babe. I'm a happy man. My life is just the way I want it. Can you say the same?"

"Mostly."

"Yeah? What about your bigamist boyfriend?" He shot her a hard look. "That make you happy, did it?"

Her bare foot tapped against the stone floor as she inhaled sharply, deeply. Then blowing the air out of her lungs in a rush, she said, "Made me happy to lock his ass up."

"Uh-huh." He turned, leaned one hip against the railing and watched her now, relishing the sparks flashing in her eyes. "And just how'd that happen? You catch him with his other wife?"

"No." She took a drink of her wine and then she was the one who shifted her gaze out to the ocean and what lay beyond. "I got a call from someone wanting to book a 'round-the-world cruise. She came to the agency to talk it over, but she wasn't there to book the trip. She had another woman with her. Both of them were Mike's wives. They showed me pictures. Marriage certificates. And they wanted me to go with them to the police to file charges."

He watched her and though her voice was clear, steady, he saw the dregs of pain and humiliation in her expression and didn't enjoy it as much as he might have thought he would. "Must have been rough."

She shrugged it off, as if it were nothing. "Rougher on them. They had kids with him. The bastard."

He picked up her wineglass, handed it to her, then took another drink himself. "Here's to lucky escapes, then."

"Yeah. Real lucky." But she drank, then shifted a look at him. "Why so interested?"

"Curious, that's all. Wondered what kind of man it was you said *yes* to."

She swallowed hard, stared into her wine as if looking there for a script to read. "I didn't want to walk away from you, Gabe."

"Really?" he asked, irony coloring his tone even as a wry smile curved his mouth. "Because you didn't seem to have any trouble with it at the time."

"We had nothing," she said quietly.

"We had everything," he argued.

She finished off her wine, then held the empty glass between both hands as if needing something to hold on to. "We were in school, still. No money, no prospects."

"We had plans," he reminded her, feeling again the long-ago sting of realizing that she hadn't believed in him.

"It wasn't enough." She pushed one hand through her hair, scraping it back from her face as she looked up at him. "Don't you get it? I told you then that I had to finish school. I needed to find a stable career. One that I could depend on. I couldn't take a chance—"

"On me?"

Her eyes filled with tears she blinked to keep at bay, but he wouldn't be sucked into feeling sympathy for her.

After a long moment or two she sighed heavily and said, "I told you about when I was a kid…"

He nodded, remembering. He'd had a family. Security. And it had been hard for him to identify with what she'd gone through, but it hadn't mattered. All that had mattered for him then, was *her.*

"About how my mom lost her job and for a while, we even lived in our *car.*" She sucked in a breath as if it were her last and said, "We had nothing. No home. No money. *Nothing.*" Turning her gaze back to the sweep of ocean, she said, "Then, later, when Mom was back on her feet and she got so sick, we couldn't afford a damn doctor." A single tear rolled down her cheek and glistened like silver in the moonlight. "I watched her die by inches, knowing that if things were different, if we'd had insurance, or savings, we could have found someone. I don't know. A specialist, maybe. *Someone* who could have helped her. Saved her."

"So you walked away from me because I didn't have money."

"It wasn't about *money,*" she said hotly. "It was about security. Stability. Easy enough for you to dismiss it when you never had to wonder if you were going to eat that day or not."

"I loved you."

"And I loved you."

"You just didn't believe in me." And that still stung. Still gnawed at him at the odd moment.

"Do you think it was easy for me to leave? To turn you down when I loved you so much?"

He turned from her and walked back into the living room because he couldn't stand beside her and not touch her again. And, damn it, he didn't want to touch her at the moment. "I think your idea of love was wrapped up in the wrong things." He spun around and faced her as she followed him. "You said yes to this Mike guy. What? He have a good job? Insurance? Savings accounts?"

"He wasn't rich, if that's what you're getting at."

"But stable?" He laughed. "A stable bigamist. Good call, Deb."

"Easy for you to throw stones, isn't it, Gabe?" She waved both arms out, as if to encompass the entire resort. "You're the king of your own little empire. What do you know about it?"

Fury exploded inside him. He took one long step closer to her then forced himself to stop. Glaring at her, he said, "Let me get this straight. When I didn't have a dime, you dumped me. And now I'm loaded and you're *still* giving me a hard time? What is your deal, anyway?"

She fisted both hands at her hips and leaned in toward him. "You never understood. You still don't. It wasn't about money, Gabe. It was *never* about money. It was about being *safe*. I never wanted money so I could run barefoot through it. I just wanted to know that the rug wasn't going to be pulled out from under me again."

"You should have trusted me," he said, his voice a low throb of old hurt and new fury. Irritated the hell out of him that this should still be bugging him. He'd thought he'd put the past and *her* behind him years ago. Apparently, though, there were still a few things that needed to be said. "Should have had faith in me. In *us*. Yeah, your life was hard, but I was there. I loved you. I would have taken care of you."

"Don't you get it?" she countered. "I needed to take care of myself."

"And how's that working out for you?"

She pulled at her hair. "You are the most irritating, frustrating man I have ever known in my life."

"And you are the most distrustful, mercenary…"

"Mercenary?"

"You heard me."

"You jerk, I just tried to explain—"

"*I'm* a jerk?" He laughed shortly. "Right. Whatever helps you sleep nights."

"You know what'll help me sleep nights?" She stepped up closer, planted both hands on his chest and shoved. Didn't budge him an inch. "Getting off this damned island."

He grabbed her wrists and held on tight. "Yeah, well that ain't gonna happen."

"Why not?" She tried to pull free, but his grip was too strong. "You don't want me here. Despite what just happened between us. So just help me leave."

No. That single word echoed over and over again in his mind. He took her chin with his fingers and tilted it up so that she met his gaze. "It's *because* of what happened between us that you're not leaving. Not yet."

"What?" She pulled out of his grasp.

"You heard me." He rubbed his fingers together as if he could still feel the touch of her face. "We don't have a future and the past is gone. What we *do* have is the present. Here. Now."

"And that's it?" she asked, shaking her head and backing away from him. "Just sex. That's all we've got?"

He speared her with a cold, hard look. "What else is there?"

"I guess you were right, after all," she said softly. "I don't know you anymore."

Seven

"What do you mean, Culp and Bergman canceled their contract?" Debbie leaped up out of her chair as if she'd been electrocuted and tried to listen to her manager's voice through the roaring of her own blood.

She'd just talked to her manager the day before and everything at home had been fine. But then again, just yesterday she'd only been Gabe's captive. Not his lover/captive. Oh, what a difference a day made.

"Just what I said, Deb," Kara Stevens told her over the phone. "The CEO's admin called this morning, said they'd decided to use another agency."

Debbie's stomach pitched and rolled. It wasn't enough that she'd spent most of the night before miserable that she was in love—*again*—with a man she had no future with. *Oh, no*. Wasn't enough that Gabe had used up her body and dismissed her heart.

Now she had to find out that her travel agency's biggest client was leaving her for someone else.

"That doesn't make sense," she sputtered, stalking around Gabe's living room.

"I know. I was totally stunned, too. Yesterday, I sent over the papers for their company cruise, just like you told me to. Everything was peaches and gravy, you know?" Kara was babbling, words tripping over each other as she rushed to get all the bad news said at once. "And then this morning, I get the phone call and they're dumping us. They didn't say why or anything, either, and I swear I didn't do anything wrong, Debbie. Honestly. Worked up the papers just like last year's, but…"

"This can't be happening." Debbie moved onto the stone terrace and stood in a slice of brilliant sunshine. She squinted against the glare and watched colorful sailboats glide across the ocean through narrowed eyes. It was a postcard kind of day at Fantasies.

Yet here in Debbie's little world, it was midnight and howling with a bitter wind.

Dread coiled in the pit of her stomach and sent cold, thick tendrils out to freeze every square inch of her body. She swallowed hard against the knot of nerves lodged in her throat. "Did they say who they were going with instead?"

"Nope," Kara answered quietly. "Just that they were through with us. God, Deb, I'm so sorry. I feel so totally bad right now, you don't even know. I mean this is just such a class-A bummer and everything…"

Bummer?

This was way bigger than a simple bummer.

Kara didn't know the half of it, Debbie thought. Without Culp and Bergman, Debbie's travel agency was going to be on shaky ground. She'd been building her business slowly over the last several years, but the corporate account she'd snagged with C and B had really been her main source of income for two years.

The fact was, there were so many people booking trips online these days, that no one thought they really needed a travel agent anymore. They were wrong, of course.

Sure you could book your own trip. But what if an airline went on strike while you were vacationing in Ireland? What if your luggage was lost in Istanbul? What if you needed an emergency ride home and couldn't *get* online?

A good travel agent could take care of any problems. She'd saved her clients all kinds of aggravation over the years. But did anyone care about that when they could just click and buy? No.

"So what do you want me to do now?" Kara was asking.

"Nothing," Debbie said, curling her fingers around the railing. There was nothing Kara could do. Heck, nothing Debbie could do, trapped as she was in la-la land. "Don't do anything until I get home."

"And when's *that* gonna be?" Kara's voice shifted from worried to complaining in a blink. "I mean, I know I agreed to manage the place while you were gone, but you were supposed to be home like a week ago, you know?"

"Yeah, I know," Debbie said as frustration churned and frothed in the pit of her stomach, making an ugly mix. She should be home right now, dealing with this. If she were, she could go to C and B herself. Get to the bottom of things. Maybe strike a deal. But no... "Something came up here and I can't leave yet."

"Until when?"

"I'm not sure," Debbie admitted, wishing she had the stupid jewel thief in front of her. She'd give that woman such a kick. "Soon, I hope."

"Well me, too, cuz I don't think I'm cut out for being the boss, Deb. This is just way too stressful."

Debbie groaned, let her chin hit her chest and rolled her eyes. Kara was nice, good with people and had a sharp eye for details. But her stress-o-meter was a lot lower than Debbie's. Kara tended to freak first, ask questions later. Of course, this was the perfect situation for a little freaking.

This went beyond problem into the scary realm of *disaster.* With a capital *D.* If Debbie couldn't get C and B back in the fold—or find another corporate client— her business would fail. She simply couldn't make a living on walk-in customers.

Now fear chewed at her insides, making the frustration she'd felt only moments ago feel like a walk in the park in comparison.

"I know," Debbie said, rubbing her forehead in an attempt to ease the sudden and ferocious pounding there. "And I'll get home as fast as I can, Kara. Trust me. You're gonna have to hold down the fort a little longer, though. Can you do that?"

"I guess…"

Filled with confidence, Debbie hung up, tucked her phone into the pocket of her jeans and tried to see past her own panic. What the hell was she going to do? She'd spent the last five years building up her business, nurturing it, growing it until it was something she could be proud of. Something she felt safe about. Something that made her feel secure in a sometimes scary world.

And now, that world had just gotten a lot shakier.

She should call C and B herself. Talk to the admin. Find out what was going on. Beg. Plead. Whine. Whimper like a kicked dog.

"Okay, not a good idea." Debbie blew out a long breath and dragged in another one trying to find calm. "I can't call her yet. I'll just wait until I'm a little more zenlike—shouldn't take more than a year or so…oh, God. I'm so dead."

Dropping into the nearest chair, she pulled her knees up and rested her chin on top of them. Her brain raced as she tried to find a solution. She could call Cait or Janine to whine. But then, her best friends would instantly offer to loan her money or whatever. And they couldn't afford it, either.

Their new fiancés could, but Debbie sooo didn't want to be borrowing money from Jefferson Lyon or Max Striver. Besides, borrowing money wasn't a long-term answer. And that's what she needed. She had to find a new corporate client. Someone bigger than Culp and Bergman. A company that would not only make her little travel agency solvent, but help it grow.

"Sure," she whispered, "no problem."

God. She rested her head against the back of the cushioned chair and stared up at the brilliantly blue sky. Twists of white clouds strung across the expanse like spools of ribbon unwinding. From a distance, she could just make out the sounds of muted music and laughter.

The land that Gabe built.

Where sunshine and sensual pleasures combine to make a magical world where troubles just couldn't find a place to roost.

Well, apparently except for *her*.

Gabe.

His name rolled through her mind, but she shook her head before the idea could take root. Stupid. Impossible. And yet… If she could arrange for a packaging deal with Fantasies, her travel agency could become the hottest agency in California. Maybe the United States.

She sat up a little straighter and stared out past the railing toward the ocean where the wind whipped white caps on waves that rolled perpetually toward a white sand beach.

People would line up at her door to get hold of an exclusive discounted package to Fantasies. She could be the only agent around to be able to offer those deals and her business would be saved.

But even as the thought rolled through her mind, Debbie was shaking her head. She couldn't do it.

Couldn't go to Gabe and ask a favor. God. How could she? She'd turned down his marriage proposal back when neither of them had a dime and now, because he's rich, she asks to use him?

Oh, no.

There had to be another way.

And she'd find it.

But first, Gabe or no Gabe, she had to get off this damn island.

Later that afternoon Deb had had enough. Fine. She couldn't leave the island because she was a suspect. She could *almost* deal with that. But she wasn't a felon *yet*. So why was a big burly security guy following her all over Fantasies? This was so not her imagination. Everywhere she turned, there he was, blending into the crowd with all the success of a redwood attempting to look like a rosebush. Not that he was trying to hide or anything, because if he was, wearing that red security jacket was a bad idea.

She made a quick right turn near the bank of elevators off the lobby and when her "shadow" showed up, she stepped out from behind a potted palm. "Okay," she demanded, "what is it you're trying to find out about me?"

He stared down at her for a long minute and Debbie momentarily regretted the impulse to face him. He was huge. And strong. With features that looked as if they were carved from stone. Until he smiled and his expression shifted into one of admiration.

"Nicely done." Even his voice was huge. Deep and rolling like thunder.

"Thanks," she said, relaxing just a bit, since it didn't look as though he was about to cuff her and throw her in a dungeon. "Now, who are you and why are you following me?"

A couple of guests approached, loaded down with shopping bags from the village shops. Debbie watched them with more than a little envy. She was trying to avoid jail and, hey, save her livelihood. All they had to worry about was their Visa bill.

When the couple disappeared into an elevator, the big man spoke up. His voice rumbled out around her and she realized exactly why he was in security. Who would try to get anything past this guy?

"The name's Victor Reyes. I'm chief of security here on the island."

"Aren't there more important things to take care of than following me?"

He shrugged. "I have my orders, miss."

So, was Gabe trying to keep her safe or was he trying to find out if she really was the stupid jewel thief? Didn't he know her better than that? Didn't their night together mean a damn thing? "And you've been ordered to follow me around?"

He only nodded.

"I'm not a thief."

"Glad to hear it, but that doesn't change my orders, miss."

"No," she said, disgusted more with Gabe than with

the poor guy just doing his job. "I guess it doesn't. But I'm going to go talk to someone who can change them."

"Mr. Vaughn isn't in his office," the big man said as she started toward the elevator.

Stopping dead, Debbie turned to look at him. Sunlight slanted in through the wide windows, splashing the red-and-white decor with a golden light. The thick, sweet scent of flowers caressed the air and under any other circumstances, Debbie would have been enjoying the ambience. As it was...

"Then where is he?"

"He's judging a surfing contest on the beach."

Stunned, Debbie couldn't even think of a thing to say. She was being treated like a criminal and Gabe was off judging a surfing contest? What had happened to his offer of help? Where was the concern? Where was the trust?

"That's just perfect," she muttered, and headed past her guard dog at a fast clip. "You don't have to follow me. I'm not going to do any permanent damage to surfer boy."

He chuckled, but fell into step behind her. She sighed, then let it go. She couldn't stop him and at least, Debbie thought grimly, he was keeping his distance.

Clearly, Gabe wasn't exactly working his tail off to help her out. So, fine. If Gabe wasn't going to help her, she'd do this herself.

She'd call Cait. Call Janine. Call the National Guard if she had to. She couldn't afford to sit around and wait for island authorities to decide she was innocent. She had to get home. Like, now.

Her sandals clacked on the tiles and her vision was

going red at the edges. Probably not helpful to be this darn mad, but she didn't see how she could help it. She hit the automatic front doors and kept walking, cutting across the neatly tended lawn, moving from sun to shadow and sun again. She hardly saw her surroundings, but she was alert enough to glance over her shoulder and note that Mr. Security was tagging along after her. "Honestly, shouldn't he be putting his efforts into actually finding the real thief?"

"What do you mean, he can't help?" Debbie's voice hitched near hysteria as she listened to Caitlyn try to calm her down.

"Jefferson's got his lawyers looking into getting your passport returned, but apparently it's going to take some time before we can clear this up."

Debbie tripped on the edge of the walk leading down to the beach and hopped on one foot as she gritted her teeth through the pain of a stubbed toe. "Well, what the hell kind of no-good lawyers does your boyfriend have working for him, anyway?"

"Way to keep calm, Deb."

"Calm?" She shot a look over her shoulder. Her own personal mountain was still following her, but he was staying far enough back from her that she could at least speak freely to her friend. "I can't believe this. I'm living in a soap opera."

"It's not that bad, honey."

Cait could only say that because she didn't know the whole story. Debbie hadn't told her about the disaster looming over her business. But heck. Wasn't the rest of this mess enough to elicit a little sympathy? "Hello? Suspect. Security guard following me around like a starving pit bull looking for a snack." The pain in her foot ebbed back a bit and she hissed out a breath. "I can't leave the island and, oh yeah, *Gabe* is my jailer."

"Yeah," Cait murmured, "that part sucks. Janine told me he still looks hot."

Hotter than he should, that was for sure, Debbie thought. Because even when she was furious with him, all she had to do was to think about him and that long, amazing night together and her blood pressure shot out of orbit. "That's not the point, though, is it?"

"No, but it could be worse."

"How?"

"Well, you could be in jail instead of Gabe's place."

"True…" Debbie sighed, stepped out of her sandals and walked onto the warm sand. It shifted beneath her feet, squeezed up between her toes and made walking just a bit more difficult. There wasn't much of a crowd on the beach, but those that were there made plenty of noise. The cheers and shouts for the surfing competitors lifted into the air and hung there like limp flags.

Instinctively, Debbie headed away from the crowd. She didn't really want to see Gabe lording it over his guests and she could hardly hear Cait when she talked.

"But staying with Gabe has its own problems," she said when she was far enough from the crowd. "And besides, I've got to get home. I've got a business to run." *Save,* she added silently. "And a supposed life to live and—"

"And it'll all be here for you when you get back. Jeez, Deb. You're in a place most people only dream about visiting. Sure, there's a couple of flies in your soup at the moment."

"Big damn flies, if you ask me," Debbie muttered.

"But the soup is still pretty fabulous."

Debbie lifted her face into the kiss of the wind and looked at the endless sweep of ocean stretched out in front of her. Sailboats, surfboards and body surfers littered the water, and on the horizon, dark clouds were gathered up like soldiers preparing an attack. She wanted to take a moment, let her worries slide away and see the upside like Cait wanted her to.

But the point was, there were much bigger flies in her soup than Cait knew. Debbie didn't have a clue what to do next. Where to turn. Who to tell what to. And in that frenzied moment of wild thinking, she heard herself blurt, "I slept with him."

"You what with who?"

"Gabe. Slept. Well…" Debbie hedged as she kicked at the sand. "Not so much slept with as rode like a pony for hours."

A humming silence filled her ear for several seconds and Debbie almost smiled as she imagined Cait's look of complete shock.

"This is huge. I can't believe you didn't tell me," Cait finally shrieked, her voice hitting a note that had Debbie yanking the cell phone away from her ear in self-defense.

"I just did tell you."

"Yeah, finally." Cait grumbled a bit, then said, "Was

it great? Was he great? Ohmigod, I can't believe you're together again."

"Whoa."

"What?"

"We're not 'together.'"

"But you're sleeping with him."

"Only the one night." Three or four times, but she didn't need to say that. Debbie quickened her pace, riding the hot flush of something sizzling through her system. She headed straight for the edge of the water and stood in the cool, wet sand. A froth of lacy, cold ocean slid up to shore, covered her feet and buried them in the sand. And still, she felt heat building inside. Gabe was way too powerful, even in memory, to be doused by a little icy water.

There was silence for a long minute, then Cait asked, "And you're okay with this?"

"Not like I've got a choice or anything, you know? Gabe's…"

"Still pissed. Yeah, Janine told me."

"It's more than that," Debbie admitted, and walked a little closer to the ocean. Now the water slapped at her ankles even as the sun poured down on her from above. "It's like he's determined to not feel a thing for me."

"Do you blame him?"

Debbie pulled the phone away, stuck her tongue out at it, then slapped it to her ear again. "Thanks, pal."

"Well, come on, Deb. Men are so easily bruised and you really crushed him back in the day."

"At the time," Debbie pointed out, "I seem to remember you telling me I did the right thing."

She swung her right leg through the water, splashing it higher. The wind kicked up suddenly and tossed her hair into her eyes.

"Of course I said that," Cait told her. "I'm your friend. That's my job."

"So you lied?"

"Well, yeah."

"I can't believe this," Debbie said tightly. "I thought you understood. You *said* you did."

Cait sighed. "I never really understood why you'd dump a guy who so clearly loved you and who you were so obviously nuts about. Shoot me. I was trying to be supportive."

"Don't tempt me," Debbie said. "And why didn't you understand? I explained it to you and Janine both."

"I know, honey, and I know you really believed it. But—"

"But?" She turned her head and stared down the beach, where the surfers were riding lazy waves to shore.

"But love isn't about security, Deb. It's about risk. About taking chances and hoping for the best."

"That's not exactly logical."

"Who says love has anything to do with logic?"

Love. She *had* loved Gabe desperately and it had almost killed her to walk away from him. But her fear had been stronger than her love and that was something she didn't like admitting, even to herself.

"You still love him, don't you?" Cait asked, then added quickly, "And don't bother to lie, because I know you too well. You don't sleep with a guy unless you care for him. And this is Gabe we're talking about. The love of your life. Your dream man. Mr. Perfect."

"The guy who wants nothing to do with me, you mean?"

"Well, yeah. There is that."

"Cait, I don't know what to do. I need to get home. I need to leave. But if I leave, I'll never see him again, I know it."

There it was. Fear upon fear. She had to go home, try to save her business. But once she left the island any connection with Gabe would be gone. And if she tried to maintain a connection, forge a business alliance, then she'd only look like she was trying to use him.

"The flies in my soup are doing the backstroke."

"Maybe it's time to toss out the soup and order something different."

Debbie choked out a laugh. "Could we stop talking in food analogies?"

Cait laughed. "Sure. All I'm saying is, why don't you actually try to talk to Gabe? Tell him how you feel."

"And give him the chance to shut me down like I did him once upon a time?"

"I said it was a risk."

Yes. But was it one she was willing to take?

Eight

Two hours later Victor Reyes was standing in Gabe's office making his report. "She's a little jumpy if you ask me."

Gabe leaned back in his desk chair, looked up at his friend. "Not surprising."

"Surprised the hell outta me that she'd confront me like she did."

Gabe smiled. He wished he'd seen her jump out from behind a palm to face down the man following her. Like a mouse standing up to a hungry cat. She'd always been confident, sure of herself. Even when she'd walked away from him ten years ago, she'd done it fast and clean, as if she'd *known* that it was the right thing to do.

Even though it hadn't been.

Damned if he hadn't missed her. Hell of a thing to be forced to admit ten years after he'd seen the last of her. But there it was. Having her here with him was supposed to be punishing her. He didn't want to enjoy her. Didn't want to want her.

"She's got guts."

"Yeah, she does. Debbie never did have a problem expressing herself."

"You might not want to hear this, boss, but I like her."

No, he didn't want to hear it. Worse yet, he didn't want to understand Victor's reasons for saying so. Frowning now, Gabe said, "Yeah, me, too."

"So when are you going to tell her they caught the jewel thief?"

"Well now, that's a good question." Gabe picked up a pen from the top of his desk and idly tapped it against the sleek, red-leather blotter. They'd gotten word just a couple of hours ago, via fax, that the jewel thief had been caught and jailed in Bermuda. Not that the arrest mattered since it wasn't the reason Gabe had held Debbie on the island in the first place. But she would expect to be able to leave and he hadn't decided just yet how to squash that notion.

"She'll hear about it soon enough. It'll make the news and even if she doesn't see it there, people talk."

He scrubbed one hand across his face, pushed his hair back from his forehead and said, "I'll worry about that when it happens."

"Your call, boss," Victor said, already turning for the door. "But if you want my advice…"

"I don't."

"Like I said. Your call." He opened the door and stopped. "You want me to keep following her?"

"No." Gabe leaned back in his chair and tossed the pen aside. "No point. Besides, maybe she'll start wondering why you've stopped."

Victor laughed shortly. "Gotta say, you two make a hell of a pair."

When he was gone, Gabe thought about that for a long minute, then dismissed it. Once upon a time, Victor might have been right. But that was long ago. Today, they weren't a pair. And Gabe had no interest in changing that fact.

Debbie paced the living room of Gabe's suite, avoiding the scattered chairs as she wound in and out. Stepping from glossy floor to jewel-toned rugs, her sandals sighed and clicked in turn.

She held the phone to her ear and hummed along to the annoying wait music playing on the line. How anyone could play an oldie rock tune like the Rolling Stones' "Satisfaction" in violins was beyond her. But so not the point.

The point, she reminded herself as her stomach jittered and her mouth went dry, was to talk to the admin at Culp and Bergman. Find out why they'd cancelled their account with her agency and see what she could do about wooing them back.

Maybe she shouldn't have called them yet. Maybe she should have given it another day. More time for her to settle. Or, on the other hand, more time for an ulcer to develop and turn her into a gibbering idiot.

"Ms. Harris?"

When an actual human voice broke into the music, it took Debbie a second or two to respond. "Yes. I'm here."

"What can I do for you?"

Frowning now, Debbie bit back on her impatience. The woman knew exactly why she was calling, but apparently they were going to play the game. But that was all right. Debbie'd been dealing with the coldly efficient Ms. Baker for two years now.

"I spoke to my manager at the agency yesterday and she tells me there's a problem with the renewal of our contract with your company."

"No problem," the woman said, her tone clipped and businesslike. "We've simply decided to go with someone else."

"Ms. Baker," Debbie said quickly, "we've worked together now for two years and I think we've done very well by each other and—"

"Yes, but times change, Ms. Harris," the other woman interrupted, her tone going even brisker. "We at Culp and Bergman felt that to meet all of our travel needs, it would be better to go with a bigger agency."

"Bigger?" She couldn't compete with bigger. That was the whole point. The fact that she was a small, independent agency had been her selling point when she'd landed the C and B account two years before. A smaller agency gave more personal attention. "Bigger isn't always better, Ms. Baker. And I think you'll have to admit that in the last two years, my agency has handled your company's work in a timely, efficient manner and—"

"Yes, of course."

The patient tone in the other woman's voice had Debbie rolling her eyes and gritting her teeth. "I should be back in Long Beach within the week—" *Please, God* "—and if you'd allow me to fax over a revised contract, I'm sure we could come to terms that would satisfy both of us."

"I'm very sorry, but a new contract has already been signed with Drifters. There's really nothing more to be said, Ms. Harris. Now I'm afraid I'm very busy, so if you don't mind, thank you for calling."

The hum of the dial tone in Debbie's ear seemed to vibrate right down to her toes. *Drifters.* One of the biggest travel agencies in the state, they were probably able to offer C and B all kinds of discount travel packages and who knew what kinds of incentives, and there was simply no way Debbie could compete with a company like that.

She was sunk. Literally. She could almost hear her business sliding down the tubes. Slowly, she closed her cell phone and wrapped it in one tight fist. Debbie felt as though she'd taken a punch in the stomach. Sort of light-headed and woozy.

She stared around the room as if she wasn't quite sure where she was. Sunlight splashed through the wide windows and lay in brilliant slices across the floor. The sheer drapes at the French doors fluttered in a wild breeze and the scent of the ocean wrapped itself around her.

Yet she hardly noticed any of it. Instead she was concentrating on breathing. Pushing air in and out of her lungs. A hard ball of ice settled in the pit of her stomach and Debbie was afraid she was going to have to learn to live with it.

Without Culp and Bergman, she wasn't going to be able to keep her company running. Unless she could find another corporate client, she would lose everything.

"Gabe will probably get a charge out of that," she muttered.

"Speaking of Gabe," a woman's voice said from right behind her. "Where exactly is he?"

Debbie spun around so fast, she caught her foot on the leg of a stupid chair, lost her balance and nearly fell face-first onto the floor before she caught herself. Staring at the gorgeous brunette watching her through curious eyes, Debbie put her at about thirty, with pale white skin, dark-brown eyes and a killer lemon-yellow silk suit. She looked like she'd just stepped off the cover of a magazine.

"Who're you?" Debbie finally said as the woman dropped her purse onto a chair.

"I'm Grace Madison and now that you know my name, perhaps you'll tell me who *you* are and what you're doing in my fiancé's suite."

Gabe looked up when a short, blond tornado roared into his office. Her long hair was flying loose around her shoulders and the pale-blue tank top she wore bared an inch or so of her tanned belly just above her white shorts. But before he could enjoy the spurt of pure lust that shot through him, he shifted his gaze to hers.

Debbie's eyes were shooting blue fire and he had no

doubt at all that if looks could really kill, she'd have him six feet under in an unmarked grave.

Being a wise man, his first instinct was to take a wary step back from a woman that furious. Instead, though, deliberately casual, he kicked his legs out, crossed his feet at the ankle and folded his arms behind his head. "Deb, nice of you to drop in."

"You *jerk.*"

One corner of his mouth quirked. Nothing quite as entertaining as Debbie in a fury. "If you're going to call me names, you might want to close my office door."

"Gaaaahhhh…" She growled an inarticulate sound, spun around and crossed back to the door. When she got there, she slammed it hard enough to have several of his framed paintings rattle on the wall.

Chest heaving, eyes bright with rage, she shook a finger at him. "You're *engaged.*"

He'd forgotten all about Grace's impending arrival. Still, it didn't change anything. He and Grace had an arrangement. One that suited them both and had nothing at all to do with Debbie Harris.

"Ah. Grace must have arrived."

"That's *it?*" she practically howled. "That's all you've got to say?"

"What would you like to hear?" he asked, straightening to lean his forearms on his desk. He watched her as she stalked back across the room and stopped just opposite him. Damn, she looked good when she was pissed. And what kind of twisted SOB was he that he wanted her right now?

"What I *want* to hear you say is that she's not your fiancée."

"She's not."

Debbie jerked upright, sucked in a gulp of air, blinked at him and said, "What?"

"Not officially, at any rate," Gabe said. "I haven't asked her yet, but unlike the last time I proposed to someone, I'm expecting a yes."

"You…you…"

"Yes?"

"You can just sit there and tell me that you're going to marry some other woman after we…we…"

"Having trouble stringing those sentences together, are you?"

"We had *sex!*"

"We surely did," Gabe mused, and stood slowly, his gaze never leaving her. The flush of rage on her cheeks, the short, sharp breaths making her breasts heave, the fire in her eyes, and the furious twist of her mouth were all combining to make him hot and hard and so damn ready for her. He didn't think he could wait another second without having her.

"You had sex with me and you're going to marry *her.*"

"Eventually," he agreed as he walked past her and continued to the door. There, he threw the lock and turned around to look at her again. "Did you think I didn't have a life before you showed up on my island?"

She scowled at him, still furious, but riding a much colder rage than she had been. "No, but—"

"Did you seriously believe there'd been no other women for me since you?"

"No. Of course not." She folded her arms over her chest and tapped the toe of one sandal against the floor.

He tipped his head to one side and studied her. Objectively, he tried to figure out just what it was about this one particular woman that got to him like no other since her. Then he dismissed that thought because it didn't matter. "Did you ever think that I didn't much care for the idea of you sleeping with your bigamist?"

"I didn't do it when I was having sex with *you*."

Gabe shrugged and started toward her. "And I haven't had sex with Grace in months."

"And that's supposed to make it all right?" Debbie backed up as he advanced but he caught the spark in her eyes. The hitch in her breath. She was as ripe as he was.

"I didn't owe you an explanation, Deb. Still don't," he reminded her, and came around the edge of the desk to grab her. "But the truth is, Grace and I made a business decision to get married."

"Business?"

He shrugged and tightened his grip on her upper arms so she couldn't slip away from him. "Neither one of us is interested in 'love' and we'd both like a family. Her family owns a cruise line…good business to have a merger."

"Well, that's cold," Debbie muttered.

"No, that's business."

"And what're we?"

"Good question."

She tried, briefly, to pull free again, but after a moment or two, she simply looked up at him. "You could have warned me that she was coming. That she *existed*."

"Yeah. I could have."

"Wow." She sighed and shook her head even as she lifted both hands to his chest to try to push him away. "That's such a great apology. You should have that sewn on a pillow."

He laughed. Damn it, nobody else had ever been able to make him laugh in the middle of a fight.

"I'm not apologizing for how I live my life."

"What about to Grace?" she demanded. "You going to apologize to her?"

"No," he said, and lifted one hand to stroke the side of her face. "She wouldn't expect an apology."

Debbie sucked in a breath at his touch and held it for a long moment before exhaling again. Then she batted his hand away. "She's a damned sight more understanding than I am."

He laughed and touched her again, dipping one finger beneath the edge of her top to stroke her bare skin. "Honey, Genghis Khan is more understanding than you."

"Funny." She glanced down at his hand, sliding down to cup her breast and even when she inhaled sharply, she blurted, "No way are we going to have sex again. Not with your *fiancée* right upstairs in your suite, so if you're thinking what I think you're thinking, you might as well—"

"Shut up, Deb," he whispered, and leaned down to kiss her. It started off slow, soft, and quickly became a kiss of hunger so raw, so basic, it stole his breath. *This* Gabe hadn't counted on. *This* he would have avoided if he could have. But damn if she didn't touch him in places he'd thought long since closed off.

And damn if Grace's arrival was going to make him stop wanting Debbie. What he and Grace had was more of a business arrangement. There was no love and therefore no cheating. And besides, they weren't engaged *yet*.

"We shouldn't do this," she said when she tore her mouth from his a moment later.

"But we are."

She looked up at him, cupped his face between her palms and said, "Oh, yeah. We are."

Then Gabe stopped thinking. He pulled her tank top off and tossed it to one side. She was yanking his shirt up and over his head and at the same time, running her palms over his chest, his abdomen. His body was hard and tight and he knew if he didn't have her in the next few seconds, he would simply explode. He'd never known such a ferocious need like he did with Debbie.

Quickly, they tore off the rest of their clothes and then Gabe was lifting her, sliding everything off of his desk and sitting her on the edge of it before moving in to tear her shorts off her body.

The desktop was cold on her skin, but she was hot everywhere else. He entered her and Debbie felt her heart stop. Felt her brain click. Thoughts slide into place and she knew, bone-deep, that *this* was where she belonged. With this man.

And that knowledge bloomed and died with an unspoken sigh, because she also knew that she couldn't have him. That he didn't love her anymore. That he never would. That the woman he was planning to marry for all the wrong reasons was upstairs and just what did that make Debbie to be down here, making love with a man who belonged to someone else?

She shut down her mind because the answer to that question was just too painful. Instead, she concentrated on the feel of Gabe's body sliding in and out of hers. On the hush of his breath, on the raging hunger ensnaring them both. Because she knew this would be the last time she would be with him. She couldn't make love with him again, knowing that there was nothing more than lust fueling it. Couldn't have him and know she would lose him.

"You're thinking again," he said, cupping one of her breasts in his palm. His thumb and forefinger tweaked her nipple and she sucked in air greedily.

"I'm stopping now," she swore as his body plunged into hers, jolting her with a pleasure so rich, so deep, it nearly brought tears to her eyes.

"Good idea," he whispered, and kissed her, taking her mouth with a fierce passion that wrapped itself around her in a silken net of desire.

She wrapped her arms around his neck, lifted her legs to hook around his hips and held on while the man of her dreams, the man from her past, made her present dissolve into a mass of shimmering light and color.

Nine

"This has *got* to stop happening," Debbie muttered as she snatched up her panties and stepped into them.

"Yeah?" Gabe laughed, reached over to slap her behind and laughed again when she shouted at him. "Why's that?"

She swung her hair back and out of her eyes and fixed him with a glare that should have set fire to him— if he'd had the slightest sense of decency! Naturally, he didn't.

Grabbing her shorts, she tugged them on, then looked around for her bra. While she searched, she sent a quick glance at Gabe. "How do you do that?"

"What?"

"Pretend everything's great. Normal. That we're just

an average couple and you don't have an almost-fiancée right upstairs."

His features went cold and stiff as he picked up her bra off the back of his desk chair and tossed it to her. "We're not a normal couple, Deb. And the fact that Grace is here has nothing to do with what's between us."

She slipped into the bra and tried to understand how he could go from blazing hot to Arctic ice in a heartbeat. Tossing her hair back from her face, she grabbed her tank top and didn't speak again until she was wearing it. "That's just so much bull, Gabe. You know it and so do I. Something's going on here between us and—"

"The only thing going on between us is sex. Amazingly good sex, but that's it."

His words slapped at her and stung like tiny darts tossed at her heart. How was this possible? How could he look right at her and *lie* so easily. Because he *was* lying. She knew it. She felt it. There was more between them than he wanted to admit. Otherwise, she never would have fallen in love with him all over again.

But if he didn't acknowledge their connection, she had nothing.

"I can't do this, Gabe. I can't stay with you, sleep with you all the time knowing that it means *nothing* to you."

"I didn't say that," he allowed quietly. "What I'm saying is that what we've got in bed together has nothing to do with my life."

"Oh, well then. *Okay.*" She staggered back a step and

stared at him as though she'd never seen him before. And this Gabe, she really hadn't seen. Didn't know. "As long as your life doesn't get disturbed then all is right with the world?" While she talked, her temper spiked and burned as though her chest was on fire.

"Pretty much," he said, and had the nerve to smile at her.

"You really are a bastard, aren't you?"

"Just figuring that out?" he said with a smile.

She took a long, deep breath and counted to ten—okay, five—before trusting herself to speak again. If all that they had was what *she* was feeling, then Debbie was finished.

"That does it, Mr. Island-Owner-King-of-the-World. I want you to give me back my passport and get me the hell off this island."

He looked at her for a long minute and Debbie realized she couldn't read any of what he was feeling in his eyes. And that hurt more than anything.

"You don't always get what you want, Deb. You should know that. Now, if you don't mind, I've got to get back to work."

Dismissing her, he bent to pick up the papers and things he'd tossed off his desktop.

Debbie, though, wasn't going to be ignored anymore. She stomped around to the far side of his desk, bent and grabbed up a stack of papers and slammed them down onto his desk with a slap of her hand. "There. Nice and tidy. So you have room to talk to me. You have time to tell me why, if you feel nothing for me, you're not working harder to get me off this island."

"Don't get it, do you?" He leaned in close until his mouth was just a breath away from hers. His gaze speared into hers and she felt a chill beneath the fury she saw pulsing there. "This was never about protecting you. This was about punishing you."

Punishing…a light began to dawn and Debbie didn't much care for it. Could she really have been so wrong about him? Did he really feel nothing more for her than a lingering fury over a decade-old injury?

"Ten years ago," he said, bringing life to her thoughts, "you used me up and cut me loose. Well, payback's a bitch, babe. And this time it's your turn."

She shook her head and stepped back from him, unwilling to be so close to the hard glint in his eyes. "You're doing all of this, keeping me here, holding me captive, just to hurt me?"

"You expected different?" he asked, standing now and shoving both hands into the pockets of his white slacks. He laughed shortly and shook his head. "Hell, if that jewel thief thing hadn't come up, I'd have found another way to keep you here just to make sure I got a little of my own back. God, Debbie, did you really think I was carrying some torch for you? That this would all end up in some Hollywood version of happily-ever-after?"

"No," she said, though damned if a part of her hadn't actually been hoping for something along those lines, despite the fact that he'd claimed to not return what she felt for him. To protect herself, she lifted her chin and lied. "I suppose you thought I was going to fall madly in love?"

"Didn't you?" he asked slyly.

Yes, she thought, but said only, "Oh, please."

He nodded, staring at her as if trying to read the thoughts racing through her mind. Finally he smiled. "Nice try, babe. But you forget, I've seen you in love. I know what it looks like on you."

Debbie squirmed uncomfortably. "We're not talking about me. We're talking about you. And from where I'm standing it seems you've gone to a whole lot of trouble over a woman you claim to care nothing about."

He scowled at her, then turned his back to stare out the window at the resort he'd built. "I don't have to explain myself to you, Deb. I've told you that before, too."

"No," she said, weary now, right down to the bone. What had begun a few weeks ago as a dream escape had slowly turned into the vacation of the damned. "But you might want to try to explain it to yourself, Gabe. Maybe ask yourself what you get out of this."

He glanced at her over his shoulder. "I get the satisfaction of keeping you here against your will."

Her jaw dropped. "Once they catch that jewel thief, I'm out of here."

"Maybe. Maybe not. This is my island, Deb." He turned to face her. "If I say you don't leave, trust me on this, you don't leave."

"Gabe, I have a *life.* A *business.* You can't keep me here indefinitely."

"Don't bet on it."

"You're not some feudal lord, Gabe."

"Might as well be, as far as you're concerned."

Debbie shook her head. "So, me being suspected of being a felon really worked out well for you, then."

"I'd have thought of something else if that hadn't happened along."

"I don't even know you anymore, do I?"

"You got that right."

"I had no idea you hated me this much."

He blew out a breath. "I don't hate you, Deb. But I'm not the guy you once ripped apart, either."

"I won't let you keep me here."

"You don't have a choice."

Debbie walked up to him and poked her index finger into his chest. "I do. I'll call the police."

"Already told you that won't work."

"I'll call my friends."

He laughed. "O-oh. Now I'm worried."

Anger shot through her and seemed to dazzle even her vision so that she was looking at Gabe and seeing him blurred out. "This is over, Gabe. This...whatever it is between us. You've had your revenge or whatever. Congrats. Kudos to you. So now that we both know where we stand, why don't you call the authorities in Bermuda and tell them I'm not the thief."

"Why would I want to do that?"

"Because it's the right thing to do."

"Oh, well then."

He walked away, turning from both her and the conversation. She couldn't believe this. Any of it. Only a few minutes ago, she'd been having sex with this man. On his desk, for pity's sake. They'd been as close as two people could possibly be and yet now, it was as if they were on different planets.

Heck.

Galaxies.

"And what about Grace?" she whispered.

"Grace is none of your business."

"Shouldn't she be yours?" she countered.

"How about you stay out of my life?"

"How about you let me get back to mine?"

"When I'm ready," he said, "not before."

"And that's when, exactly?"

"When I'm tired of you."

Debbie sighed, fought past the pain, the humiliation of the moment, and tried to gather up the fast-unraveling threads of her mind. When she thought she could speak again without shrieking, she tried reason on him. "Look, Gabe. I don't just want to leave. I have to. My business is in trouble," she added, though it galled like hell to have to admit this to him of all people. "If I don't get home and do some damage control, I could lose everything."

He sat behind his desk, leaned back in the chair and folded his hands atop his abdomen. Tipping his head to one side, he studied her as he asked, "What seems to be the problem?"

She swallowed hard. God, wasn't it bad enough that she'd been humiliated already? No, it wasn't. Because until they caught that stupid jewel thief, Gabe was the only guy who could convince the authorities that she was innocent. Not that it looked as though he was in any hurry to do her any favors…but she had to try. Keeping her voice level, she tried not to feel the sting of failure as she said, "I lost my corporate client."

God, it sounded hideous when she heard it said out loud. "I've got to find a replacement for them because the walk-in business isn't enough to keep it going. And my assistant can't handle it on her own, because she doesn't know the business like I do and besides, the responsibility for the agency is all mine, anyway, and—"

"So let's see if I understand this," he mused, cutting off her stream of consciousness. He sat up straight, then leaned his forearms on the desktop. "Ten years ago, you walked out because I had nothing. Because you wanted 'security.' Now, I've got all the security you ever dreamed of and more and you've got—what? A failing business? A bigamist fiancé? That about sum it up?"

Debbie lifted her chin and narrowed her eyes on him. "Fine. Yes. You're fabulous and I'm a loser. Is that what you needed to hear? Now are you happy?"

"You have no idea what I'm feeling," he said quietly.

"So why don't you tell me, Gabe." She walked toward the desk, planted both hands on the edge and leaned in. "You're the one keeping score. You're the one who keeps dragging our past up to throw it in my face. Why don't you tell me what you're feeling right now? Get it said. Then maybe we can both move on."

There was a slow sizzle of temper in him. That was easy enough to see. His green eyes flashed and his mouth worked as though he were biting back words fighting to get said. For a couple of tension-filled seconds, Debbie was sure he would say exactly what was on his mind.

Then the moment passed and a shutter dropped over his eyes even as he shook his head and said, "I've got work. As a 'businesswoman,' you should appreciate that."

"Right." She nodded and stepped away from the desk. Away from the man who was behaving as if she'd already left his office. "I'll let you get to that, then."

She walked to the door and looked back at him. He was ignoring her, but she knew he was still paying attention. "This isn't over, Gabe. I'm going to get off this island. With or without your help."

A few hours later Debbie took a seat at the bar, ordered a raspberry martini and while she waited for her drink, let her gaze sweep the crowded casino while her freaked-out mind took a little break. After all, she'd been doing nothing but trying to think of a way out of this situation for *hours.*

And while she was all tense and tied up in tight little knots, the rest of the crowd gathered at Fantasies looked to be having a great time. Elegant couples in tuxedos and jewel-toned gowns drifted across the glossy floor, sat at gaming tables and fed hungry slot machines. The ceiling was shot through with neon and flashing lights in dizzying bursts of color that pulsed in time with the rock music pumped through stereo speakers high on the walls. The air fairly shimmered with a party atmosphere and Debbie, watching them all through tired eyes, felt like a balloon with a slow leak.

Torn between hurt and anger, she wasn't sure what her next move should be. She could call Janine or Cait. Involve the police. Heck, call the United Nations or something. The Marines! Do whatever she had to do to get off this stupid island and away from Gabe.

But was she willing to have Gabe arrested to make her escape? "Yes."

No.

Not really. It wasn't as though she hated him or something. She *loved* him. Not that that was doing her any good. The big jerk.

So, she thought, let's recap. Held prisoner by an ex-lover. Trapped on an island paradise. Suspected of being an international thief. About to go into bankruptcy.

"Yep. Been a hell of a month so far," she muttered, and somehow managed to keep from banging her forehead on the bar.

"Sounds like you need this," the bartender said, sliding her drink toward her.

"You have no idea." Automatically she reached for her purse, but the bartender shook his head. "No charge for you, Ms. Harris. Boss's orders."

She smiled, though inside she was quaking. The boss. He did like giving orders. And taking charge. And holding hostages. And…

"Is this seat taken?"

She turned her head and looked up at Grace, Gabe's almost-fiancée. The woman was gorgeous in a dark-red gown that clung lovingly to generous curves. Even in her own sapphire-blue dress Debbie felt like the ugly stepsister at the ball.

Well, isn't this a perfect end to a perfect day, she thought.

Grace watched her coolly, as if she knew exactly what Debbie was thinking. And why shouldn't she?

"No, feel free," Debbie said with a half smile, and waved a hand at the stool beside her.

Grace slid onto it, signaled the bartender and ordered champagne. While she waited, she turned to Debbie and said, "I thought we should talk."

Ten

Smiling, Grace nodded at the bartender when he delivered her drink, then she picked up the crystal flute and took a sip. "Ah. That's better."

Might've been better for her, but Debbie was feeling a little antsy. After all, what could she possibly say to the fiancée of the man she was in love with? Debbie groaned and winced inwardly. She could hardly believe herself that she was still in love with a man who was virtually holding her prisoner. Could there be a more awful moment?

Grace sat on her bar stool, crossed her legs and took another sip of champagne while watching Debbie over the rim of her glass. There was something very like amusement flickering in the woman's dark eyes and

Debbie took a slightly less flustered breath before speaking.

"So, this is awkward."

"Not as much as you might think," Grace said, still holding her champagne flute in one graceful hand. "I understand that you and Gabriel have become quite the item."

"I didn't know about you," Debbie told her.

Grace shrugged. "Nor I you. But I did speak with Gabriel."

"Really?" Debbie watched the other woman and wondered out loud, "What'd he have to say?"

"That you two are old…friends."

"I suppose that's true." Debbie sipped at her martini, paused a moment and said, "I want you to know something. Before I came here, I hadn't seen Gabe in ten years. I don't want you thinking that we've been having an affair or something right under your nose." She took a deep breath, then a long drink of her raspberry-flavored liquor. "A. I would never do something like that, I'm just not that kind of person, though I guess from your perspective, you might not believe me on that. But Gabe wouldn't do it, either, and you probably know him well enough to believe that, because you are going to marry him, so of course you know him, though not me, at all, I mean. I'm a stranger who can't seem to stop talking…"

"Is there a 'B'?" Grace asked when she paused for breath.

"I can't remember."

"Doesn't matter, really. I only came to see you to let you know I'm leaving."

"Because of me?"

"Please." The woman chuckled and shook her head. "No. While Gabriel is certainly a diverting man…"

Oh, diverting was a good word for it.

"I've decided to marry someone else. I only came here because I wanted to tell him my decision in person."

Yikes. "How'd he take it?"

"Quite well." She gave Debbie a quick but thorough up and down look. "With you here, he's obviously otherwise occupied, anyway."

"Look, Gabe and I…"

"Are none of my business," Grace said, taking another sip of her drink. "I'm going to be married in three months."

"Congratulations." Debbie had one fleeting thought, wondering what kind of man would be interested in tying himself forever to a woman who seemed chillingly cold. And then wondered if Gabe realized what a lucky escape he'd had.

She couldn't imagine Gabe married to this woman. He was so easygoing, so, enjoy-life-every-minute. Well, he used to be. As she'd found out all too recently, she really didn't know this new Gabe very well at all. From what she'd seen of the man Gabe had become over the last few days, maybe Grace was exactly the kind of woman he wanted.

"Thank you." Sliding off her bar stool, Grace stood,

smoothed one hand down the front of her gown and gave Debbie a brief smile. "Now, I'll say good-night. Oh," she added as she turned to leave, "good luck with Gabriel."

While the crowded casino hummed with activity and sound, it was as if a small bubble of silence had been erected around the two women. Neither of them was aware of anything going on in the background. Each of them was instead focused on the odd situation they found themselves in.

"I don't have Gabe," Debbie pointed out.

Grace quirked her head to one side and said, "Well, good heavens. You love him, don't you?"

Debbie stiffened. "Oh, let's not go there."

"This is surprising."

"You're telling me." Seriously, could there be a weirder conversation? How hideous it was to be in love alone. Even with all she and Gabe had said to each other in the last few days, she knew that a part of her would always miss him. Ten years ago, she'd walked away, thinking she had known what was best—for both of them.

Leaving Gabe then had nearly killed her—but now it was going to be so much worse. She was older now. Knew more about herself and what she wanted—needed. And she knew that losing Gabe this time was going to haunt her for the rest of her life. Yet there was nothing to be done about it.

"You got a gorgeous women you're holding captive on this island and you're sitting here having a drink with me," Victor said on a short laugh. "What's wrong with this picture?"

Gabe scowled at his friend, tossed back the last of the Scotch in his glass and asked, "Don't like my company?"

Victor leaned back into the sofa in his suite of rooms and stared at his boss. "Didn't say I was complaining, just wondering why you're here instead of with your blonde?"

"She's not *my* blonde."

"What about Ms. Madison?"

"Gone," Gabe said, and didn't want to admit even to himself that he was relieved about Grace leaving the island. Hell, until he'd found Debbie again, he'd been willing to settle for a loveless "arrangement" of a marriage. But once he'd felt the fire again, the thought of marrying Grace had become an impossible one.

Just as well she'd found another man.

Gabe reached for the bottle of Scotch sitting atop a coffee table and splashed more of the amber liquid into the crystal tumbler. How his pal could be confused as to why Gabe would rather be here, drinking with a friend, rather than talking to the woman currently making him insane, was beyond him.

Studying the Scotch like a man looking for answers in all the wrong places, Gabe was remembering the look on Debbie's face as she'd walked out of his office. He could still clearly see the hurt, and it shocked him that he wasn't enjoying this more.

Hey, mission accomplished. He'd set her up and knocked her down. So why the hell wasn't he celebrating?

Damn woman never should have come back into his life. He'd had it all a few short weeks ago. He'd been happy.

He took a long drink before saying, "To answer your question, the reason the blonde came to mind first is, she's the one irritating me at the moment."

"Uh-huh, and how's she doing that?" Victor asked. "Complaining about being held prisoner, is she?"

Flashing the other man a dark look, Gabe demanded, "Whose side are you on, anyway?"

"Yours, boss." Victor held up both hands in mock surrender.

"Damn straight. Somebody sure should be." Gabe kicked his legs out in front of him, crossed his feet at the ankles and glowered into his glass of Scotch. Didn't seem to matter how much he drank. He couldn't wipe Debbie's image out of his mind. And he wanted to, for God's sake.

He didn't owe her a blasted thing.

"Saw Grace heading into the casino a bit ago," Victor said.

"Yeah?" Jesus, he was being a miserable bastard.

"Your blonde's in there, too. Thought you should know the two of them looked like they were going to be comparing some notes."

"Great." With the two women talking, God only knew what would happen next. Lifting his gaze to his friend's, Gabe asked, "Just how did my life go down the toilet so fast?"

"Man," Victor mused, setting his own glass of Scotch onto the table, "what makes you think your life was so great before all this happened?"

Gabe squinted at him. "It was. Everything was fine before Deb showed up."

Victor laughed shortly and shook his head. "You didn't notice that whenever Grace arrived you got suddenly busy?"

"No." He took another drink of Scotch, letting the liquor slide down his throat in a fiery trail.

"Well, I did." Victor took a sip of his own drink, sighed and said, "Not that Grace went looking for you much, either. Seems to me, if you're going to marry somebody—even if it's a business arrangement—folks usually want to spend some time together."

"What's your point?"

"You know my point."

Gabe blew out a long breath. Yeah, he knew what his friend was talking about. Hadn't wanted to think about it, and still didn't, come to that. But Victor was right. He and Grace had had an arrangement for a marriage that both of them were settling for—though neither of them was exactly anxious for it.

Probably hadn't been a good idea in the first place, Gabe allowed silently. No point in getting married unless you were in love, and he sure as hell wasn't in love—or planning to be.

"My point is, since the day that curvy little blonde showed up on Fantasies, you've been different."

"Like hell." A little tense maybe. A little pissed, and who could blame him? But he was still the same ol' Gabe. Debbie hadn't affected who he was at all. She was his past. That's all she was.

"Say what you will, boss, but the blonde got to you like nobody else I've ever seen."

He didn't care about Debbie. And hadn't for a very long time. "You don't know what you're talking about. I told you from the beginning that this was a game. To set her up. None of it meant anything."

"Then why're you still so pissed off when you should be happy?"

Just the question he'd been asking himself. And he still didn't have an answer. Didn't need one. "Doesn't matter."

Victor stood, looked down at his boss and said, "If you say so. But I'm wondering something."

"If I'd known you were going to be such a talker tonight, I'd have gotten drunk in my own damn room," Gabe muttered.

Victor only laughed. "No, you wouldn't. You're here trying to avoid the blonde, remember."

True. He'd come to Victor's suite looking for a friendly ear and a little peace and quiet.

"Damn women muck everything up," Gabe said, and took another sip of Scotch. "Debbie. Grace." He shook his head then let it fall against the back of the chair. "I had a great thing going here, Vic. Built my world just the way I wanted it to be. Worked damn hard for a lot of years to make this place what it is today."

"Yeah. You told me once. When you and the blonde broke up, you set out to make a fortune."

"And I did it," Gabe said, lifting his glass in a toast to himself.

"You did. But you gotta wonder…"

"What?"

"Well, if the blonde hadn't made you so damned mad all those years ago, would you be here now?"

Gabe grumbled a little, sat straighter and eyed his chief of security. "Why wouldn't I be?"

Victor shook his head and shrugged. "Not saying you wouldn't be. Only said that the blonde pissed you off enough to work your ass off to build this place. This life. Who knows where you'd be if she'd said yes ten years ago."

Frowning, Gabe stared at his drink, then reached out and set it down onto the coffee table. Thoughts tumbled through his mind as he considered Victor's words and tried to weigh them honestly.

"I'm going to head downstairs," Victor said. "Do a sweep of the place. Check in with my guys. You stay as long as you like, boss, and I'll see you later."

"Yeah." Gabe hardly noticed his friend leaving but when the other man was gone, Gabe wandered over to the French doors leading to a small balcony off the living room of the suite. He opened them, pushing them wide and was instantly slapped in the face by a fierce wind sweeping in off the ocean.

That sharp breeze seemed to scatter the fog in his mind and as he looked out at the kingdom he'd built, Gabe had to ask himself if Victor had been right. If Debbie hadn't cut him loose ten years ago, would he have had the same drive and determination to succeed? If they'd been married when he'd asked her, how much different would their lives be now? Would he even be the man he was?

He liked to think so. Liked to believe that he would have accomplished all that he had with or without the motivation of the anger she'd churned in him so long ago.

But the simple truth was, he didn't know.

Gabe had used his anger to fuel him. He'd channeled his hurt and fury into a single-minded goal. Succeeding. Making himself into the kind of man that Debbie would never have considered turning down.

So really, without Debbie...he very well might not be the king of his own little island.

"And ain't that a kick in the ass?"

"He was *engaged?*"

Janine sounded so outraged on her behalf, Debbie wanted to reach through the phone line and give her friend a big hug. Instead she settled for grumbling. "Yes. To this super-elegant, absolutely gorgeous woman."

Two hours after leaving Grace in the hotel casino, Debbie was back upstairs in Gabe's suite, pacing the room frantically, as if she could actually walk away from here if she just put enough energy into each step. Calling Janine had been grabbing onto a life rope in a churning sea. But, hey, that's what friends were for, right?

"That's so evil, I can't even come up with anything sufficiently cutting to say," Janine admitted. "What was Gabe thinking? I mean, he's all over you and neglects to mention the fiancée?"

"Technically, not a fiancée," Debbie allowed, and why she was trying to make the situation sound better was beyond her. "An almost-fiancée who is now the fiancée of somebody else, anyway, so that's over really and I don't know why I'm still freaked about it but—"

"Breathe," Janine ordered.

Debbie walked across the living-room floor and opened the French doors onto Gabe's terrace. Instantly the ocean wind slapped her in the face and forced a breath into her lungs. "Right. Right, I'm a little over the top."

"Yeah," Janine agreed. "Just a smidge."

"The worst part, though," Debbie said, leaning on the balcony railing and closing her eyes to the wind, "is that the ex-fiancée was absolutely right about something."

"Which is…"

"I'm in love with Gabe." Oh, God. She'd actually said it. Out loud. And now that it was out there in the universe, there was no pulling it back again.

"Well, to coin a phrase, *duh.*"

"Huh?"

"Honey," Janine said, her voice dropping into a soothing, sympathetic tone, "you've been in love with Gabe for like, *ever.* Pretending you weren't didn't actually change anything, you know?"

Janine was right, Debbie thought, and let her chin hit her chest. She'd always loved Gabe. Even when she'd broken it off with him, refused to marry him and hurt both of them desperately, she'd still loved him.

It was only her fears that had gotten in the way.

But wasn't it too late to do anything about that now?

"Deb?" Janine prompted. "You still there?"

"Yeah," she said softly, going back inside while leaving the terrace doors open to the night air. "I'm here. I'm just not sure where *here* is, exactly."

Eleven

A few hours later Gabe was still considering everything Victor had said. All the thoughts that had been stirred up. And he wasn't happy about it, either.

He'd like to think that he would have made a success of himself without the fury he'd felt at Debbie driving him. But the truth was, Gabe admitted ruefully, he'd never really know for sure.

He shoved one hand through his hair, swiped his card for his private elevator and when it arrived, got in. He had at least come to one conclusion tonight, despite trying to drown his thoughts in too much Scotch.

He was damned relieved Grace had called off their "arrangement." How the hell could he marry one woman while dreaming about another? He wasn't saying he was in love with Debbie, but damn if the woman wasn't still in his blood.

When the elevator doors opened, he stepped into his suite, glanced around the dimly lit room and finally spotted Deb, curled up sleeping in a dark-red chair near the now cold fireplace. Her head was tucked into the wing of the chair, her eyes were closed and her long blond hair fell softly about her face.

Something inside him twisted and though he didn't want to admit it, Gabe knew he had to let her go. For both their sakes. She needed to get back to her life and he needed her away from him. Better for both of them if they just forgot all about the last week or so.

He walked closer, his steps nearly soundless on the rug-strewn floor. He stared down at her and when his heart gave a twinge, he told himself it was nothing more than the echoes of memory. It was the past coming back to give him one more ache. One more kick. To remind him that he never should have started this little game.

Outside, the wind keened and the sheer white drapes hanging across the open French doors danced and writhed like ghosts somehow chained to the earth. The scent of rain came in on the wind and he moved to close the doors before the storm arrived.

When they were latched, he heard Debbie ask from behind him, "What's going on?"

"Storm blowing in." He turned, looked at her as she pushed herself to her feet and fought the instant, almost primal reaction he felt inside. She looked soft, and vaguely disheveled, like she'd just rolled out of bed and he wanted her in *his* bed. *Now.* Didn't matter how often they came together. How much he touched her. He knew in that one blinding moment that he would *always* want her.

That's why she had to go.

"Pack your stuff," he said suddenly, shoving both hands into his pants' pockets. "You're leaving."

"What?" Her eyes popped open wide as she stared at him.

"You. Leaving."

"When?"

"Tonight. Tomorrow. Whenever."

"Just like that?" She came around the edge of the chair and walked toward him, stopping just a few feet away.

A small distance, but it might as well have been miles.

"Now you're complaining because you can go?" He forced a laugh that felt like it was strangling him. "A few hours ago, you were demanding to leave."

"And you said I couldn't because the jewel thief hadn't been caught."

"I lied."

"What?"

He pulled a folded piece of paper from his pocket and silently handed it to her. Gabe watched while she unfolded it and quickly scanned it. When she lifted her head to glare at him, he met that cold stare with one of his own.

"You knew," she said. "You knew earlier today that the authorities caught that jewel thief in Bermuda." She stopped, took a breath and accused, "Were you *going* to tell me?"

Gabe shrugged. "No. I wasn't. Not yet, anyway."

"What is *wrong* with you?" she shouted, and balled up the paper in one fist before throwing it at him. The crushed paper bounced off his chest and onto the floor.

There was more than anger in her eyes. There was hurt and the sting of betrayal. "Because I didn't want you gone yet."

"Why?" She whispered the word. "You at least owe me that much. Why?"

"You already know the answer to that."

"Right," she said, nodding slowly. "To punish me. So why are you telling me this now? Letting me go now?"

Why did she have to look so damned good? Why was her voice so soft, her eyes so wide and beautiful? Why did he keep remembering how good they used to be together?

And why didn't he just stick to the subject at hand?

He shrugged, pulled his hands from his pockets and crossed his arms over his chest. "What difference does it make? You want to leave. I want you gone. We finally agree."

"Why the big change of heart all of a sudden?"

"God, you're like a pit bull with a bone."

"And that's not an answer."

"You want an answer? Here it is. Game over, that's all. I'm done with you and I want you gone."

She actually winced and he felt an answering ache inside him. Just another reason for her to go. He didn't want to feel for her. Didn't want to care what she was feeling, thinking.

"So the king has spoken."

"Basically."

"Great." She scraped her hands up and down her arms as if she were suddenly cold. "So you've gotten your jollies, kept me prisoner here long enough that my business will probably go belly-up and—"

He jumped on that statement. "You haven't changed a bit, you know that?" He stopped, looked at her for a long second as a small, niggling doubt took hold in his mind. "Is that why you really came here?"

"What're you talking about?" Her voice was tight, strained, as if she were desperately trying not to shout.

"You. Your precious business. Your thing with security above all else." He smiled, but it felt like more of a grimace. "You *knew* I owned this place when you came here, didn't you?"

"Oh, sure." Nodding, she looked at him as if he'd grown a second head. "I deliberately set myself up to be held prisoner."

"Why not?" He was thinking now, one thought after another screaming through his brain, and the more he thought of it, the more it all made a twisted sort of sense. "Your business was in the toilet before you came here, wasn't it? Hell, that's *why* you came here. You were going to use me to save you."

"I *what?*"

"Why else?" He asked the question, but didn't expect an answer. Now that this had occurred to him, it all made a sort of bizarre sense. And, hey, no more twinges of guilt for him. She'd come here with a purpose. He'd just been able to use her before she could use him.

He shoved his hands through his hair, scraping it back from his face before letting them fall to his sides again. "You figured to somehow cash in on our past to save your future."

"Are you crazy? I didn't know you were here. I didn't know my business was going to get into trouble. I didn't—"

"And I'm supposed to believe you?"

"Why wouldn't you?" Debbie argued. "Have I once asked you for anything except the right to *leave?*"

He didn't want to hear it. Didn't want to believe that she was telling the truth. It was easier to tell himself that Debbie had tried to run her own scam.

"You've been playing me since the beginning." It made sense. It was logical. And besides, if it were true, then he really did have nothing to feel guilty about.

"You're not serious about this."

"Oh, yeah," he assured her, "I am."

"Then I'm a bigger idiot than I thought I was."

The expression on her face was a blend of disappointment, regret and anger. Her eyes shone with unshed tears and he was coward enough to be grateful she was holding them back. He didn't want to see her cry. He didn't want to know he'd hurt her. Didn't want to have to regret another thing about Debbie Harris.

He just wanted his life back.

The way it had been before she'd returned and made him think about what-might-have-beens.

"We're done, Deb. Let it go."

"Right. You know what, Gabe?" she said finally, her

voice so soft it was almost lost in the howl of the wind slapping at the windows. "I feel sorry for you."

"Oh, please."

"I do. You've got everything you ever wanted," she said, waving both hands to encompass the suite, the resort, all of it. "But you can't see beyond it. You think I'm the one who's focused on success? It's you now, Gabe. All you can think about is this place."

"And that makes me different from you how?"

"Because I wouldn't use you—and you did use me." Her bottom lip quivered, but she made a steely effort to firm it. "You lied to me. Made me think I was about to be arrested. Held me against my will. Took me to bed and made me think—" She stopped suddenly and then added again, "You used me."

He walked toward her and stopped within arm's reach from her. He closed his hands into fists at his sides to keep from grabbing her, because damn if he didn't want to be holding her. "We used each other."

"You keep thinking that," she said with a slow shake of her head. "But the truth is, all of this was your doing, Gabe. I would never have asked you for anything for my business. See, I discovered something while I was here. I wasn't going to tell you—God knows it surprised the heck out of me. But now, I want you to know. Want you to know that this time, it's you walking away."

Looking into her eyes tore at him, but he told himself that it was all an act. She'd come here to use him, and she was pissed she hadn't been able to pull it off. "Say what you have to say, then."

"I love you."

He choked out a short laugh and felt those three words slam into what used to be his heart with a force that rocked him on his heels. He kept his expression blank, his eyes shuttered, despite the fact that he felt as though he were reeling. "You expect me to believe that."

"Nope, I don't. Like I said, it surprised me, too, when I realized it. You haven't exactly been Prince Charming over the last week, in case you hadn't noticed. You're irritating, infuriating and downright cranky most of the time. And for some strange reason, I love you anyway, so color me stupid. If you think I'm thrilled by this, you're way wrong. Especially at this moment," Debbie said, shaking her head again as she stared up at him. "I don't expect anything from you, Gabe. I just wanted you to know. Ten years ago, I walked away—and it's something I've always regretted. But today, you're the one turning your back and I want you to remember that."

"Fine. I'll remember." Damn if he didn't know that this moment would replay over and over again in his mind for years. But he'd learn to live with it. Because he wasn't going to take a chance again. Wouldn't allow himself to love again.

"Now," he asked, "don't you have some packing to do?"

"Yeah. I do," she said. "I'll pack and leave in the morning."

"Great."

"Fine."

He stared at her and told himself to take a long look

because once she'd left the island, he wouldn't be seeing her again. So he carved her image into his brain. Her sleepy eyes, her lush mouth, her tumbled hair and the thin strap of her tank top dipping off one shoulder.

And the echo of three little words still hung in the air between them like a tattered pennant that neither warring army could claim.

Debbie woke up to a furious storm rattling the windows. The wind shrieked under the penthouse eaves and whistled as it spun around the edges of the building. She stared out the windows openmouthed and watched tall, somehow elegant palm trees bend nearly in two. Their lacy fronds were tattered and torn by the force of the storm and rain lashed at the resort as if heaven had been storing water for decades only to dump it in one fell swoop.

"So," she murmured. "No leaving today."

She turned around and looked at the empty suite and wondered, not for the first time, just where Gabe had spent the night. He'd left the suite at the end of their latest blistering argument and she wondered if he'd gone looking for female company.

"Isn't that a lovely thought?" She tells him she loves him and he heads off to find anyone else. What a fabulous life she was leading. And now, she was in a storm that looked like the one Dorothy and Toto had starred in.

The resort tower almost seemed to sway in the buffeting winds and a chill snaked quickly along Debbie's spine. This couldn't be good.

When the phone on the bar rang, she nearly sprinted across the room to grab it. "Hello?"

"You okay?"

"Gabe. Yeah. I'm fine. Where are you?"

"In my office. I stayed here last night."

Ridiculous to feel the relief that was sweeping through her. But there it was.

"Your flight's been cancelled," he added unnecessarily.

She turned around to look out the windows across the room from her and said, "Yeah, I figured that out. What's going on?"

"Hurricane," he said. "Was supposed to pass us by, but it looks like its shifting direction."

Scowling, she said, "You knew I wouldn't be able to leave, didn't you?"

"What?"

"That's why you were so accommodating last night." She should have known Gabe wouldn't give in so easily. "You *knew* the hurricane was coming."

"What am I, a weatherman, now?" he argued. "For God's sake, Debbie, believe it or not, you're not at the top of my list of worries at the moment."

"What's going on?" she asked, forgetting about the spurt of anger as she reacted to the concern in his voice.

"I've got a hotel full of people to protect. People who want to get off the island almost as much as you do, and nobody's going anywhere."

"Can I help?"

There was a long pause, as if he were surprised by

the offer. Then he said, "Yeah. You could, actually. The staff is gathering up the guests, taking them into the main club room. It's the most easily protected. If you could help keep people calm…"

"I'll go now," she said, tearing her gaze from the wind-whipped scene outside.

"Thanks. I appreciate it."

"You're welcome."

And all it had taken, she thought, for the two of them to be polite to each other was a natural disaster.

Gabe lifted both hands for quiet and waited while the muttering and shouting slowly died away. He couldn't blame any of these people for being a little on the hysterical side, but it surely wasn't helping the situation any. Then he looked out over the crowd of people and started talking. He kept his voice pitched just a bit over normal, knowing that people were more likely to keep quiet in an attempt to hear him.

"I know you're all anxious and you'd like to leave…"

"The storm isn't here yet," a man in the back of the room shouted. "Why can't the planes leave before it arrives?"

Several others took up that refrain and Gabe was forced to wait again until they all settled down.

"The airfield was closed late last night as the winds began gaining in strength. The planes left while they still could."

"We're *trapped,* you mean?" A woman's voice carrying the rising edge of hysteria called the question out.

"Not trapped," Gabe said, smiling widely now, hoping to instill confidence. "Stuck. But at least," he added, "you're here at Fantasies, where your comfort is the main concern. We've got plenty of supplies. The hotel staff will be setting up cots here in the club and the chefs will keep us all well fed. All we really have to do is settle in and wait it out."

"For how long?" another man at the side of the room said.

Gabe spotted him and aimed a look right at him. "For as long as it takes. The weather reports still aren't sure exactly where the hurricane is heading. At the moment, it could keep on course for Fantasies or sheer off."

"And if it hits here?" a woman demanded, and Gabe sighed.

He searched the faces of the people looking to him for reassurance. These people were his guests. They'd come here to his home, looking for some fun, relaxation and a good time. Now they were being forced to face something none of them wanted to think about. And they were his responsibility. It was up to him to keep them all safe and calm and as happy as possible.

"If it hits," Gabe said, keeping his voice easy, casual, "then we'll deal. The resort is as safe a place as you'll find. And we're going to make it safer."

"How?" A few people shouted the single word.

"We'll be boarding up the windows in here," he said, waving one hand at the busboys who were already carrying in sheets of plywood and the tools they needed to safeguard the wide windows.

A murmur of discontent swept the crowd and he knew they were all thinking about being shut up inside a single room for who knew how long. It was going to be hard enough being part of a crowd confined in one room. But when that room had boarded-up windows and became more or less a plush jail cell, it was going to be even harder.

He was just trying to figure out a way to make this seem less frightening when someone stepped up beside him on the small stage.

Stunned speechless, he could only stare as Debbie lifted both hands and smiled at everyone. She looked happy, relaxed and completely in control.

"Hi, everybody," she said, and instantly the crowd quieted. "I know you're all nervous, but really, you don't have to be. Fantasies is safe. Mr. Vaughn and his staff are going to be doing everything they can to make this whole situation as easy as it can be on all of us."

"Who the hell're you?" A deep voice from the back of the room sounded out.

"My name's Debbie Harris," she said, speaking slowly and clearly. "I own a travel agency in California and I can tell you firsthand, I've been in situations just like this one in far less favorable circumstances and I'm still here to tell the tale."

Someone laughed nervously and while Gabe watched with interest, Debbie kept talking. "I'm going to be helping Mr. Vaughn out as much as possible."

She glanced at Gabe and shot him a smile bright enough to light up every shadow inside him. Admiration for her filled him and he had to admit that the feel of the crowd had really eased up since she'd joined him on the stage. There was just something about her that reached people.

Including him.

"I'm a guest here, too," Debbie was saying. "Just like the rest of you. I know none of us signed up to work on our vacations, but I've found that keeping busy in stressful times helps us all to feel safer. And, if we all work together, we can get through this with as little trouble as possible."

There was some muttering, but mostly, Gabe noticed, the people in the crowd were more relaxed. Some of them smiling, some of them nodding. All of them listening.

"Now, if some of you guys would go to the windows and help the busboys with the plywood, that'd be great," Debbie said. As a few men moved off, she continued. "And we can use more help, setting up the cots, arranging a temporary kitchen—" she looked at Gabe and he pointed to the far corner "—over there. We'll need people to help serve, set up chairs, to pass out supplies, make lists and, oh, lots of other stuff."

She grinned at them all again, as if she and the crowd were sharing a secret and Gabe saw just how well it was working. Before there had been nerves, fear and a humming energy that could have turned ugly. But in just a few minutes Debbie's easy smile, professional savvy and knowledge of human nature had turned it all around.

"So how about it?" she asked. "You guys willing to pitch in?"

Applause started, slowly at first, and then catching on and rising into a wave of sound that roared into the closed-up room. And while the guests cheered, Gabe looked at Debbie and felt his heart turn over.

Twelve

The storm raged all day and long into the night.

Debbie became the unofficial cruise director—initiating games, sing-alongs, even, in desperation, a marshmallow roast over the chef's open flames. She'd done anything she could think of to keep the crowd relaxed. She hadn't had a moment to just sit all night.

Gabe and his staff had been just as busy.

Silently, efficiently, they went about the business of keeping everyone safe. The windows were boarded, security guards were on hand to keep people from stealing outside to watch the storm and Gabe himself seemed to be constantly in motion. She watched him work the crowd, smiling, chatting as if this was just another weekend on Fantasies. His easy manner and quiet confidence instilled a sense of well-being in everyone he passed and Debbie had to admire him for it.

Gabe really was in his element, she realized. This place was more than his kingdom. It was his *home* and here, he was both host *and* touchstone.

Wandering the darkened room, Debbie walked around the edge of the club, moving as quietly as she could. People were stretched out on the cots and mats provided by the hotel, and some of them were even managing to sleep, in spite of the howling wind and the rain slamming against the boarded-up windows. A few muffled sobs reached her, too, and she knew that fear was still high as the world outside seemed to tear itself apart.

All she really wanted was a place to collapse. She was bone-weary but too wired to sleep. Besides, she didn't think she'd be able to close her eyes while the wind was screaming like some wild creature just outside the room.

Grabbing a cup of coffee from the chef's table, she held it between her palms and carried it with her to the far side of the club. There, she gratefully eased down to the floor and leaned against the wall.

Sipping at her coffee, she tried not to listen to the storm. Tried to ignore the hundred or more terrified people in the room. Tried not to let her own fear, that she'd been successfully blocking all day, suddenly take up life in the pit of her stomach. She tried, anyway.

"Mind some company?"

Debbie looked up at Gabe and shook her head. "Not at all. Pull up the floor and sit down."

His mouth quirked into a half smile as he eased down

beside her. Pulling one knee up, he rested his forearm atop it and stared off across the room. "Long day."

"Yeah, it really was." She took a sip of coffee, then held the cup out to him.

"Thanks." He took a sip, sighed, then handed it back to her. "And not just for the coffee."

"You're welcome," Debbie said, then laughed a little. "Wow. We're actually being nice to each other twice in one day."

He leaned back, stretched out his legs and folded his arms over his chest. "A record for us."

"Didn't used to be." Debbie looked at him, his profile softened in the dim light, and her heart filled with both want and regret. "There was a time when we were great together."

"A long time ago."

In the dark, in the relative quiet in their little corner of the room, she said softly, "I didn't want to say no to you ten years ago, Gabe. I loved you so much."

He turned his head to look down at her, but with the light behind him, she couldn't really see his eyes. And she wished she could. She'd always been able to look into those eyes and see love.

God, she missed that.

"You should have had faith in me, Deb," he said, and his voice sounded tired. "Faith in us."

"Maybe," she admitted, thinking back to the girl she had once been. The girl who had been so scared. Scared of loving too much. Scared of never being safe. Scared of taking a chance—a risk. "Maybe I should have,

Gabe. I don't really know anymore. But since we're being so honest here, do you think you'd have done all this if we had stayed together back then?"

"Funny," he said after a long moment or two. "Someone else asked me that just yesterday."

"And?"

"And, I don't know." He blew out a breath. "Guess I'll never know. I was so damn mad at you for so long…"

Blindly, she reached for his hand and when his fingers closed over hers, Debbie clung to the warmth of him as he continued. "I loved you then, Deb. Enough that it almost killed me when you walked out."

"Gabe—"

"But I won't love you again."

Debbie's heart broke at his quiet words because she knew they would never have the second chance together that she wanted so much. Maybe the brass ring really did only come around once in a lifetime. And if you missed your shot at it, then it was just too bad for you.

"We got lucky," Gabe said late the next morning as he studied the windswept grounds stretched out in front of him. "If the hurricane hadn't veered off sometime last night, we'd be in much worse shape."

"I suppose so," Debbie said from right beside him. "But, Gabe, everything looks…"

He knew what it looked like. A war zone. Trees had broken and lay splintered across the ground like toys discarded by a petulant child. The pools were filled with dirt and leaves and God knew what else. Awnings were ripped, signs torn from their posts.

But there hadn't been any injuries, so he called it a win.

And now that the storm was over, it was time to get things back to normal. All the way around. He blew out a breath. "We'll get it cleaned up within the next few weeks. But with any luck, the airfield should be clear in a couple of days. You can catch the first plane out."

She was quiet for a long moment, then said, "All right."

He turned and looked down at her. They'd come through the storm and having survived it, they were both a little stronger, a little more sure of themselves and a little further apart. That bothered him a hell of a lot.

He'd seen her in action and knew what an amazing woman she really was. When things were toughest, Debbie had come through. Having her with him had made everything easier. She'd helped him when he needed it most and now that she was leaving, he could do the same for her.

Even things out between them as best as he could.

Then they'd each have a clean slate. No guilt. No…unfinished business.

"There's something else," he said, his gaze locked with hers.

All around them, the resort was slowly coming back to life. Workers hustled, cleaning up debris, guests staggered out of the main club like shipwrecked survivors getting their first glimpse of land, and the sun spilled down on all of them.

"What is it?"

"You came through for me during the storm—"

"You already thanked me," she said quickly.

"This is something else." He smoothed a strand of her hair back and tucked it behind her ear. "When you get back to Long Beach, I want you to draw up a plan—a travel package plan. Fantasies will offer discounted vacations through your company."

She took a step back and stared at him in stunned amazement. "Gabe, are you sure? That's *huge*. Why would you do that for me?"

Because he didn't want to worry about her. Because he wanted her dreams to come true. Because maybe she and Victor had been right and he really wouldn't have had this success without the nudge she'd unconsciously given him ten years ago.

"It's good business," he hedged, not wanting her gratitude. "We'll get guests we might not have had otherwise and the packages will save your company."

"More than," she said. "I'll be the only travel agent in the country with a packaging deal for the most sought-after resort in the world."

He gave her a half smile and shrugged. "Good business. Like I said."

Reaching out one hand to him, she whispered, "Gabe…"

He took her hand, squeezed it, then let her go. "I've got to get to work." He walked off, then stopped and said, "You can stay in the suite till you leave. I'll bunk in my office."

He left her standing there amid the rubble that had once been his only dream.

And he didn't dare look back.

"He did *what?*" Janine demanded.

Debbie gripped her cell phone a little tighter and told her friend about Gabe's offer again.

"That's amazing, girl," Janine said with a low whistle of appreciation. "Okay, I'm feeling a little more charitable toward good ol' Gabe again. This'll make your little agency the hottest one in the state. Maybe the whole country."

"I know." Debbie wandered through Gabe's suite and stepped out onto the terrace. The suite was too empty without him. And knowing that he'd be avoiding the place until she was gone only made it—and her—feel emptier.

Below, the golf course was looking a little wind-blown, but she could see teams of employees out there now, working to bring it all back to rights. Everyone on Fantasies had been working like maniacs all day to restore the resort to its pre-hurricane splendor. It might take a few weeks to get it all back to what it had been, but she didn't doubt for a minute that Gabe would pull it off. Heck, he'd probably make improvements and have Fantasies even better than before.

The man was unstoppable.

"You're not jumping up and down with excitement."

"I should be," Debbie agreed, tilting her face up into the sunlight. "This is the answer to everything. It's more than I'd even hoped for."

"Yet…"

She smiled at Janine's coaxing tone.

"Yet," Debbie said with a sigh, "this packaging deal with Gabe just doesn't seem as important to me as it once would have been."

"Because you've got your much-loved security but you don't got Gabe?"

"Nice grammar, but yeah," Debbie admitted. "That's about the size of it."

"Well, yippy-skippy," Janine said with a hoot of laughter. "It's about time."

"So happy to amuse," Debbie said, frowning at the phone in her hand. "Care to explain?"

"Love to—" Then Janine broke off, held her hand half over the receiver and called, "Max, *please* don't help the movers, you'll break that lamp and—" The sound of splintering glass came through the phone just before Janine sighed. "Never mind."

"Which lamp?" Debbie asked, smiling as she opened her eyes and stared out at the horizon.

"The glass one with the faux Tiffany shade."

"Bummer."

"Yeah, well, Max is great, but careful he's not. Sorry, honey." The sound of a kiss came across the line, then Janine was talking again. "Okay, Max is outside, directing the movers, which I'm sure they totally appreciate, so now back to you."

"Oh, goody."

"Hey," Janine reminded her, "you wanted the explanation, remember?"

"Fine," Debbie said, and dropped down to the stone floor to sit. No point in trying to sit on one of the chairs. The red-and-white cushions were waterlogged and filthy. At least the stone floor had had enough time to dry out. Besides, she didn't want to be inside, in that empty suite. "Explain why you're so pleased with my misery."

"Not your misery, Deb. But I'm loving the epiphany."

"I didn't mention an epiphany."

"Sure you did, you just didn't recognize it. Think about this," Janine continued in an oh-so-patient tone. "You've got the deal of a lifetime. One that'll not only save your business but probably make you stinking rich, right?"

"Yeessss…"

"You've got built-in security. Even enough for you, my slightly crazy friend."

"Thank you so much, but, yes, I get what you're saying and I still don't see the epiphany."

"Here it is. You've got security, but it doesn't mean anything without the love."

She groaned. "Janine…"

"Deb, security's overrated."

"So says someone who's never lived in her car."

Janine ignored her. "It's good, sure, but you can't count on it. Life happens, Deb. Businesses rise and fall. Don't you get it? The only *real* security is love. The kind of love that doesn't let you down. The kind you can count on no matter what else happens in this wide, weird, crazy world. That's the only security that's worth a damn, girlfriend. And, I think you've finally figured that out."

Everything her friend said chimed inside Debbie like

a clear bell of truth. Hadn't she pretty much come to these same conclusions in the last twenty-four hours herself? Hadn't she already felt the hard fact that even with a Fantasies contract, without Gabe, she would never be truly happy?

Was it all so easy, then?

So simple?

"Hello?" Janine said. "You still there?"

"Yeah," Debbie answered, her voice little more than a whisper. "I'm here. And I get it. I love Gabe."

"Yep."

"But how could he ever believe that I love him for himself and not for what he's become?"

Not surprisingly, Janine didn't have an answer. And *that,* Debbie thought, was the saddest part of all. She loved a man she couldn't have. A man she'd had and lost ten years ago. A man who only the night before had told her flat-out that he wouldn't love her again.

Two days later Debbie was at the airfield. The place still looked ragged but the runway was open and planes were lined up on the tarmac, waiting to take weary passengers home.

She turned her back on the field and looked at the road leading to Fantasies. To where Gabe was. It seemed like years since she'd first arrived here, determined to have the vacation of a lifetime.

Now she was going home and so much was different. She'd found Gabe and lost him again. Her business had crashed and then risen like a Phoenix. She'd survived a hurricane and had had an epiphany much too late to change anything for the better.

Now, she had to leave, though she'd never wanted to do anything less. But in this, she was as trapped as she had been when Gabe had first captured her. She had to leave because he'd never believe she was staying for the right reasons.

Heck, she hadn't even said goodbye to him. What would be the point? They'd already said everything.

A blurred voice came over the loudspeaker and Debbie listened to it with a heavy heart. That was her flight and she'd run out of reasons to stay on the island. Tearing her gaze away from the road that would lead her back to Gabe, she turned and headed for the boarding gate.

A half hour later the small commuter plane had its engines up and running for the short flight to Bermuda. From there, Debbie would catch her flight to LAX. Once home, she'd start trying to put Gabe behind her.

Again.

"I apologize, ladies and gentlemen." The soft, smooth voice of a flight attendant carried over the plane's loudspeaker. "There will be a slight delay in our takeoff time."

"What now?" someone muttered.

A woman two rows up from Debbie started crying, the sound quickly escalating into a wail. Apparently nerves were still frayed from the hurricane.

The flight attendant forced a smile as the door behind her was wrenched open and said, "Someone else is boarding, it will take a few minutes to sort things out. I do apologize, but ask you to be patient."

Debbie couldn't have cared less. She stared bleakly out the small porthole window at the tarmac and the island beyond and tried not to think about all she was leaving behind.

"Debbie!"

She blinked, turned her head and stared up the long, narrow aisle. Gabe stood at the front of the plane, sweeping his gaze across the faces of the passengers until he spotted her. Then, with long, hurried strides, he headed to the back of the plane. Everyone watched him, spinning around in their seats so they wouldn't miss a thing.

"Gabe?" She looked up at him as he stopped in the aisle beside her seat. "What're you doing?"

"You're getting off this plane."

"No, I'm not," she argued, and slapped at his hands when he reached down to undo her seat belt.

"You're coming with me."

"Stop this!" She snapped her belt shut again when he flipped the latch. Then he undid it again and she sighed. "What're you doing, Gabe? Just stop, all right?"

"Miss," one of the passengers, a tall guy with a sunburn, said from across the aisle, "do you need some help?"

Gabe shot him a murderous look and said quietly, "Stay out of this."

"Gabe." Debbie's heart pounded hard in her chest and a sheen of tears blurred her vision. "You can't make me leave this plane. Besides, haven't we said enough? Haven't we already hurt each other enough?"

All around her, her fellow passengers seemed to take a collective breath and hold it, clearly unwilling to miss anything. Debbie, though, could only stare into Gabe's eyes, wondering why he was putting them both through a goodbye scene that could only cause more pain.

Keeping her gaze locked with his, Gabe deliberately calmed himself, then held on to her forearms and pulled her to her feet. "I'm not letting you go."

"Gabe—" One wild, sputtering sparkler of hope went off in her bloodstream but she was afraid to nurture it.

"No," he said, cutting her off and ignoring the interested crowd watching him. His gaze moved over her face and Debbie felt that look like a touch. "I thought I could do it. Let you go. Live without you. I thought that's what I *wanted*. But the past couple of days have been hell, Deb. And knowing you were on this plane, about to fly out of my life forever, damn near killed me."

A female passenger sighed heavily.

Debbie couldn't spare the breath to sigh. "Gabe—"

"No." He cut her off neatly. "Just listen for a minute, okay?"

She nodded, unable to speak anyway.

"Maybe you were right ten years ago, I don't know anymore. Maybe we weren't ready. But we're sure ready now, Deb."

"Are we?"

Looking down at her, he said, "Of course we are. You love me. And I love you."

She blinked, smiled and felt a single tear slide down her cheek. "You do?"

"Hell, you know I do, Deb." He lifted both hands to cup her face in his palms. "You've always known. Why the hell else would I kidnap you?"

That same woman sighed again, a bit more dreamily this time.

"Ten years ago, I asked you a question…"

"Yes…" She waited, wanting to hear him ask that question again. Now that she was ready for him. For the life they could build together, she wanted to give him the answer he'd expected so long ago.

"This time, I'm not asking," he said. "I'm *telling* you. Get off this plane and marry me."

"Excuse me?" Not exactly the kind of proposal most women dreamed of, but looking into his eyes, she knew it was exactly the right one for her. Not that she was going to let him know that.

"You heard me," he said with a smile. Taking her hand, he turned and started back down the aisle toward the open door. "We're getting married. Today. Now."

Someone started applauding and a moment later others joined in. The flight attendant was smiling and a hearty cheer went up from the people on the plane.

Debbie stumbled after him. "At least let me get my luggage back!"

He stopped dead and Debbie plowed into him. But his arms came around her like steel bands and when he lowered his head to kiss her, bending her over double, she felt her heart do a hard gallop and everything else inside her go into a slow melt.

When he lifted his head, he winked at her. "Trust me when I say you're not gonna need your clothes."

Somebody whistled and the applause reached a thunderous roar as Gabe stood, tucked his arm around Debbie's waist and lifted her off her feet. Then he looked at the plane's passengers and said, "Give your names and addresses to the flight attendant. To apologize for the flight delay and to celebrate my marriage—" He grinned and gave Deb a quick kiss. "You're all invited back for a week's stay at Fantasies. On the house."

As the celebration roared out around her, Debbie planted both hands at the small of Gabe's back. She grinned and waved to everyone on the plane as he carried her off to their new life together.

A life where they would make *every* day a Fantasy.

* * * * *

Melita had been expecting a chaste quick kiss of the generic variety. But this kiss with Sully was the kind that sparked a dying flame to life. The kind of kiss you can't plan for. The kind of kiss memories are built on.

The memory of her murdered lover, Nemo, came to her then and she made a starved little noise in the back of her throat. She raised her arms and threaded her fingers through Sully's hair, pulled him closer. Felt his body settle, then melt into her.

In that instant her hunger for him grew, and his for her. She pressed herself to him with more urgency, and he responded in kind.

Melita came out of her kiss-induced memory of

Nemo with a start. "Wait a minute." She pushed Sully away from her. "You bastard!"

She spit two nasty words at him in Greek, then wiped his kiss from her lips.

"I thought you deserved some solid proof that I'm still in one piece." He started for the door. "The clock's ticking, honey. Come on, let's get out of here."

"That's it? You sucker me into kissing you, and that's all you have to say?"

"I'm sorry. How's that?"

He didn't sound sorry in the least. "You're—"

"Getting out of this godforsaken prison cell. Stop whining and let's go."

"Not if I was being shot at sunrise. Go. You deserve whatever you get if you walk out that door."

He turned back. "Freedom is what I'm going to get."

"A second of freedom before the guards in the hall shoot you." She jammed her hands on her hips. "And to think I was worried about you."

"If you're staying behind, it's no skin off my ass."

"Wait! What about our deal?"

"You just said you're not coming. Make up your mind."

"Have you forgotten we need a boat?"

"How could I? You keep harping on it."

"I'm not going without a boat. And those guards out there aren't going to just let you walk out of here. You need me and we need a plan."

"I already have a plan. I'm getting out of here. That's the plan."

"I should have realized that you never intended to

take me with you from the very beginning. You're a liar and a coward."

Of everything she had read, there was nothing in Sully Paxton's file that hinted he was a coward, but it was the one word that seemed to register in that one-track mind of his. The look he nailed her with a second later was pure venom.

He came at her so quickly she didn't have time to get out of his way. "You know I'm not a coward."

"Prove it. Give me until dawn. I need one more night to put everything in place before we leave the island."

"You're asking me to stay in this cell one more night...and trust you?"

"Yes."

He snorted. "Yesterday you knew they were planning to harm me, but instead of doing something about it you went to bed and never gave me a second thought. Suppose tonight you do the same. By tomorrow I might damn well be in my grave."

"Okay, I screwed up. I won't do it again." Melita sucked in a ragged breath. "I can't leave this minute. Dawn, Sully. Wait until dawn." When he looked as if he was about to say no, she pleaded, "Please wait for me."

"You're asking a lot. The door's open now. I would be a fool to hang around here and trust that you'll be back."

"What you can trust is that I want off this island as badly as you do, and you're my only hope."

"I must be crazy."

"Is that a yes?"

"Dammit!" He turned his back on her. Swore twice more.

"You won't be sorry."

He turned around. "I already am. How about we seal this new deal?"

He was staring at her lips. Suddenly Melita knew what he expected. "We already sealed it."

"One more. You enjoyed it. Admit it."

"I enjoyed it because I was kissing someone else."

He laughed. "That's a good one."

"It's true. It might have been your lips, but it wasn't you I was kissing."

"If that's your excuse for wanting to kiss me, then—"

"I was kissing Nemo."

"What's a nemo?"

Melita gave Sully a look that clearly told him that he was trespassing on sacred ground. She was about to enforce it with a warning when a voice in the hall jerked them both to attention.

She bolted away from the wall. "Get back in bed. Hurry. I'll be here before dawn."

She didn't reach the door before he snagged her arm, pulled her up against him and planted a kiss on her lips that took her completely by surprise.

When he released her, he said, "If you're confused about who just kissed you, the name's Sully. I'll be here waiting at dawn. Don't be late."

Romantic
SUSPENSE

**Sparked by Danger,
Fueled by Passion.**

Onyxx agent Sully Paxton's only chance of
survival lies in the hands of his enemy's daughter
Melita Krizova. He doesn't know he's a pawn in the
beautiful island girl's own plan for escape. Can
they survive their ruses and their fiery attraction?

*Look for the next installment in the
Spy Games miniseries,*

Sleeping with Danger

by Wendy Rosnau

Available November 2007 wherever you buy books.

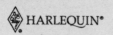

HARLEQUIN®

INTRIGUE®

WHITEHORSE MONTANA

Love can be blind...and deadly

On the night of her best friend's wedding, Laci Cavanaugh
saw that something just didn't seem right with Alyson's
new husband. When she heard the news of Alyson's
"accidental" death on her honeymoon, Laci was positive
that it was no accident at all....

Look for

THE MYSTERY MAN OF WHITEHORSE

BY B.J. DANIELS

*Available November
wherever you buy books.*

Mediterranean NIGHTS™

Not everything is above board
on Alexandra's Dream!

*Enjoy plenty of secrets, drama and sensuality
in the latest from Mediterranean Nights.*

Coming in November 2007...

BELOW DECK

by

Dorien Kelly

Determined to protect her young son,
widow Mei Lin Wang keeps him hidden
aboard *Alexandra's Dream* under cover of
her job. But life gets extremely complicated
when the ship's security officer, Gideon Dayan,
is piqued by the mystery surrounding this
beautiful, haunted woman....

REQUEST YOUR FREE BOOKS!

2 FREE NOVELS PLUS 2 FREE GIFTS!

Passionate, Powerful, Provocative!

YES! Please send me 2 FREE Silhouette Desire® novels and my 2 FREE gifts. After receiving them, if I don't wish to receive any more books, I can return the shipping statement marked "cancel." If I don't cancel, I will receive 6 brand-new novels every month and be billed just $3.80 per book in the U.S., or $4.47 per book in Canada, plus 25¢ shipping and handling per book and applicable taxes, if any*. That's a savings of almost 15% off the cover price! I understand that accepting the 2 free books and gifts places me under no obligation to buy anything. I can always return a shipment and cancel at any time. Even if I never buy another book from Silhouette, the two free books and gifts are mine to keep forever.

225 SDN EEXJ   326 SDN EEXU

Name	(PLEASE PRINT)	
Address		Apt.
City	State/Prov.	Zip/Postal Code

Signature (if under 18, a parent or guardian must sign)

Mail to the **Silhouette Reader Service™:**
IN U.S.A.: P.O. Box 1867, Buffalo, NY 14240-1867
IN CANADA: P.O. Box 609, Fort Erie, Ontario L2A 5X3

Not valid to current Silhouette Desire subscribers.

Want to try two free books from another line?
Call 1-800-873-8635 or visit www.morefreebooks.com.

* Terms and prices subject to change without notice. NY residents add applicable sales tax. Canadian residents will be charged applicable provincial taxes and GST. This offer is limited to one order per household. All orders subject to approval. Credit or debit balances in a customer's account(s) may be offset by any other outstanding balance owed by or to the customer. Please allow 4 to 6 weeks for delivery.

Your Privacy: Silhouette is committed to protecting your privacy. Our Privacy Policy is available online at www.eHarlequin.com or upon request from the Reader Service. From time to time we make our lists of customers available to reputable firms who may have a product or service of interest to you. If you would prefer we not share your name and address, please check here. ☐

SDES07

ATHENA FORCE
*Heart-pounding romance
and thrilling adventure.*

History repeats itself...unless she can stop it.

Investigative reporter Winter Archer is thrown into writing
a biography of Athena Academy's founder. But someone
out there will stop at nothing—not even murder—to
ensure that long-buried secrets remain hidden.

ATHENA FORCE

Will the women of Athena unravel Arachne's powerful
web of blackmail and death...or succumb to their
enemies' deadly secrets?

Look for

VENDETTA
by *Meredith Fletcher*

*Available November
wherever you buy books.*

COMING NEXT MONTH

#1831 SECRETS OF THE TYCOON'S BRIDE—
Emilie Rose

The Garrisons

This playboy needs a wife and deems his accountant the perfect bride-to-be…until her scandalous past is revealed.

#1832 SOLD INTO MARRIAGE—Ann Major

Can a wealthy Texan stick to his end of the bargain when he beds the very woman he's vowed to blackmail?

#1833 CHRISTMAS IN HIS ROYAL BED—Heidi Betts

A scorned debutante discovers that the prince who hired her is the same man who wants to make her his royal mistress.

#1834 PLAYBOY'S RUTHLESS PAYBACK—
Laura Wright

No Ring Required

His plan for revenge meant seducing his rival's innocent daughter. But *is* she as innocent as he thinks?

#1835 THE DESERT BRIDE OF AL ZAYED—
Tessa Radley

Billionaire Heirs

She decided her secret marriage to the sheik must end…just as he declared the time has come to produce his heir.

#1836 THE BILLIONAIRE WHO BOUGHT CHRISTMAS—
Barbara Dunlop

To save his family's fortune, the billionaire tricked his grandfather's gold-digging fiancée into marriage. Now he discovers he's wed the wrong woman!